THE SECRET BABY RESCUE

TEXAS HOTLINE SERIES, BOOK #2

JO GRAFFORD

ACKNOWLEDGMENTS

A big thank you to my beta readers, Mahasani and Auntie Em, plus my amazing editor, Cathleen Weaver. I also want to give a shout-out to my Cuppa Jo Readers on Facebook for reading and loving my books!

ABOUT THIS SERIES

Welcome to the Texas Hotline, a team of search and rescue experts — police officers, firefighters, expert divers, and more. In an emergency, your sweet and swoon-worthy rescuer is only a phone call away.

CHAPTER 1: THE EXIT

HUNT

Fourteen months! That was how long Hunt Ryker had been stuck at the specialized burn unit in San Antonio. Fourteen months of surgeries, treatments, and physical therapy sessions. Fourteen months of technically still being in the military, though he'd been forced to watch his buddies continue on without him while he assumed his new position on the sidelines. Fourteen whole months of his life that he was never going to get back.

And now the Marines were sending him home.

Home. It was only temporary, of course. Ex-Marine sergeants didn't simply move back in with their parents at the age of twenty-eight to veg out and play video games for the rest of their lives. He'd already warned them that he only planned to stay a couple of weeks, just until he could get back on his feet and take care of a few basics — like securing a new job and figuring out what came next.

He glanced around his small barracks room in the medical out-processing unit, knowing he wasn't going to miss the tiny, cave-like room with its sparse furnishings. The moment he found a new place of his own, he was yanking his personal belongings out of storage — stuff like his king-sized bed with its crazy comfortable mattress, his wide screen tv, and his humongous coffee maker with all of its cool settings. Like him, everything he owned was big. *Texas big,* as his mother liked to say.

With a grimace, he folded away his desert camouflage jacket and trousers and stuffed them in one of his three large duffel bags. It felt weird to not be wearing them any longer, and even weirder to realize he'd never be required to wear them again. Nope. He fit squarely in the category of soldiers whose services were no longer needed. Thanks to the many injuries he'd received in the line of duty, he was being medically discharged.

"You ready, Staff Sergeant?"

Hunt glanced up at Corporal Miller, one of the hospital's staff duty drivers, and nodded. It was a lie, of course. They both knew he felt about as settled as a worm in hot ashes. The only career he'd ever wanted was being cut short at the ten-year mark, and he had no idea what he was supposed to do with the rest of his life.

"Here, let me grab a couple of those bags for you, Staff Sergeant." Without waiting for an answer, the young corporal swaggered farther into the room on his two perfectly uninjured legs and reached for Hunt's duffel bags with his perfectly uninjured arms.

"Corporal Miller, attention!"

Though visibly startled, the junior soldier didn't question the order. He snapped to the position of attention with his back held stiffly upright, his arms straight at his sides, and his hands curled into fists against his thighs.

"At ease," Hunt growled, reaching for the first of his three duffel bags.

The soldier immediately switched his stance, spreading his legs about a foot apart and holding his elbows at ninety-degree angles with his hands behind his back.

Hunt wasn't normally one to use his authority to go on power trips, but standing this nobly deter-mined young soldier at attention seemed like the only sure-fire way to avoid his unwanted assistance.

Corporal Miller's worried gaze relaxed to a twinkle as he watched Hunt shrug on all three duffel bags — one over each shoulder to hang behind him and the third one looped over his biceps to hang in front.

"Carry on, Corporal," Hunt growled. He was a little embarrassed at how long it had taken him to load up his bags. Once upon a time, he could've tossed them on in a few seconds flat. But he was moving slower these days, after multiple surgeries to his once-mangled legs. Every day was a little better than the last one, but he had a long way to go to reach a full recovery.

"Yes, Staff Sergeant." Corporal Miller's voice exhibited a suspicious hitch, which made Hunt briefly close his eyes.

Lord God Almighty, give me strength. He was about to do the single toughest thing he'd ever done in his career — walk away from his job as an active duty Marine. Once outside the gates of the post, he would no longer be a soldier. The last thing he needed right now was anyone's sympathy.

Clearing his throat, the corporal stepped across the threshold and muttered something to someone on the other side.

Great. We have company. Hunt hoped it wasn't someone he knew. He wasn't in the mood for any last-minute chitchat or final goodbyes. He just wanted to leave the hospital and be done with it. Chapter closed.

To his surprise, the hall was lined with silent onlookers when he exited his barracks room. *What the—?* There were men and women in uniform, stretching down the hallway as far as he could see.

A sharp command was given. "Attention to orders!"

The hall became deathly silent as everyone present straightened to their full height and stood shoulder-to-shoulder against the walls. Although Hunt was no longer in uniform, he stood to attention in the entrance of his barracks room, more out of sheer habit than for any other reason.

"As witnessed by all those present," the same voice boomed, "this is to certify that the President of the United States of America has awarded the Purple Heart, established by General George Washington at Newburgh, New York, August 7, 1782 to Staff Sergeant Hunt Ryker, for wounds received in Action during Operation Enduring Freedom in Kandahar, Afghanistan on March 29..."

Hunt's vision blurred as the voice went on to describe in greater detail the injuries he'd suffered during the ensuing explosion. There was no way he could explain to anyone how his actions had been more practical than heroic. Since he'd been closer to the blast, he'd figured — in a snap second decision — that he wasn't likely to survive, so he'd used his body to shield another soldier, hoping to increase the chance that they both would. In the end, both of them had lived; but only one had been able to return to duty. Not him. His injuries had been too substantial.

He felt, rather than saw, the medal being pinned to his shirt — the only part of it the giver could reach above his large duffel bag. Hunt blindly returned the man's salute before continuing his walk down the hallway. The clapping of his audience rang in his ears and followed him to the sidewalk outside.

A gleaming white Ram Classic with a quad cab was idling at the curb. It was his truck, and his father was standing beside it.

Blinking away the dampness in his eyes, he limped toward the truck, pausing only when he was close enough to toss his duffel bags in the back. "I thought I told you not to come." After fourteen months of surgeries and convalescing, during which time his parents had made dozens of trips from Dallas to visit and check on him, they'd been through enough — more than enough.

"Are you kidding?" Dean Ryker exploded. He pushed back his Stetson, revealing dark eyes as damp as his son's. "Once they called and told me about the award ceremony, wild horses couldn't have dragged me away. Booked my plane ticket during the same hour."

Hunt shrugged and limped around to the driver's side of the truck. "I didn't know they were doing it, and I probably wouldn't have bothered you with the news if I had." He opened the door and swung himself behind the wheel with a smothered oomph of pain.

"Bothered!" His father cried, leaping into the passenger's side of the truck. "Ain't nothing bothersome about my son receiving a Purple Heart." He folded his long, lean, jean-clad frame into the cab and clicked on his seatbelt.

Hunt curled his upper lip as he threw his truck into gear. "Whoever decided it was a good idea to hand out an award for being injured should have his head examined," he growled. An injury wasn't the same thing as an accomplishment, for crying out loud. In many cases, it amounted to the exact opposite!

"Well, it was George Washington who made the decision, according to the very nice speech your company commander gave," Dean Ryker retorted mildly. "And in your case, it was a very grateful nation who decided to honor your sacrifices with the award."

"Can we talk about something else?" Hunt glanced in his rearview mirror at the chirp of a police siren behind him. *Are you serious?* A military police (MP) vehicle was right on his tail, lights flashing like it was Christmas. With a snarl of immense irritation, he pulled to the curb.

However, the police car neither pulled behind him nor stopped. Instead, it zipped around his truck and slowed. The driver rolled down his window and beckoned for Hunt to follow him.

Now what? Still grumbling beneath his breath, Hunt nosed his truck back into the lane and followed the MP.

More sirens sounded, and more lights flashed. To

his amazement, a line of MPs formed behind him. Five, six, seven cars joined the line, and more kept coming. It slowly dawned on Hunt that his fellow military police officers were providing him a police escort to the checkpoint. They weren't about to ticket or frisk him; it was simply their way of honoring his final exit from post.

Wow! Hunt found himself blinking back tears for a second time that morning, then was furious with himself all over again for being such a crybaby.

"I tell you what!" his father exclaimed in sheer amazement as he swiveled around to watch the cars through the rear window. "My son is a blasted war hero, and everyone around here seems to know it!"

I'm no hero, Dad. Why couldn't he see that? The real heroes were his buddies, Marcus Zane and Digby MacLamore. They'd given their all and were never coming home. "I asked if we could talk about something else," he reminded.

"Well, sure, son, if you can ignore the fact that we're right smack in the middle of a parade in your honor." He pulled out his cell phone and started snapping pictures. "I can't wait to send these to your mother."

As they reached the exit gate, the police car in front of them pulled to the side of the road and halted. The soldier inside leaped out and saluted Hunt as he drove past.

He saluted back and had to swallow hard to

avoid breaking down altogether. It was super cool of his MP buddies to do this for him. Although he hadn't asked for any attention, or wanted it, or felt like he deserved it, he'd be sure to thank them.

"Where is Mom, by the way?" Though Hunt hadn't wanted his parents to make yet another three-hundred-mile trip south for his benefit, it was a bit odd that his mother wasn't present, come to think of it. His parents were normally like two peas in a pod. They literally went everywhere together.

"With your sister." His father cast him a sideways glance. "As you can imagine, it's been a difficult time for Jillian and the baby."

By difficult, his father was referring to how Hunt's sister had gone into labor prematurely when her husband went missing in combat. As a result, Hunt's little nephew, John Tyler, whom everyone adoringly called JT, had been born early and spent the first five weeks of his life fighting to survive in a NICU. And ever since, he'd dealt with one medical setback after another.

Hunt rolled down his window to wave one last time to the crowd of MPs behind him. They responded with a flood of honking that made him grin despite the dampness in his eyes. "Now that I'm leaving the hospital, you can quit trying to protect me from the truth."

He mashed his foot against his gas pedal, putting pavement between him and his military police escort. "I know JT's been having a hard time. How bad off is he? For real, Dad?"

His father clenched his square jaw and shifted his tall, rangy frame uncomfortably on the seat cushion. For a moment, he reflected every bit of his Apache heritage, from the stoic set of his features to the grim determination in his gray gaze. "We weren't trying to keep anything from you, son. We just didn't want to cause you any extra worry." His voice was gruff. "You've had enough to deal with already the last several months."

Hunt snorted disparagingly. Flipping on his blinker, he switched lanes to pass an upcoming semi-truck trailer full of baying cattle. "She's my baby sister, Dad. She'll always be mine to worry about."

"I know." His father gave a heavy sigh. "Here's the latest and not so greatest from the home front. Our little peanut is having tubes put in his ears. His doc said this is what it's going to take to fix all the ear infections. Just wish I could believe 'em this time." He shook his head. "They keep making promises, but he never seems to get well."

Hunt nodded. He could only imagine how hard it had been on his parents during the past year, having their only son in a hospital three hundred miles away while their only grandson beat a steady path to the local emergency room.

"Things are gonna get better soon, Pop," he assured in a lighter voice than he felt.

"Oh, yeah?" Dean Ryker raised weary eyebrows. "Why's that?"

"Because I'm on my way home, which means you're about to have another set of hands to help out. It also means your corn hole partner is back for a long overdue guys-versus-gals rematch. You should probably text Mom to warn her and Jilly they'd better start preparing for the butt whooping they're about to receive."

His father gave a whoop of delight, which took some of the melancholy out of the air.

They spent the rest of their road trip listening to country music and shooting the breeze about sports.

As they approached the outskirts of Dallas, his father gave a loud groan of frustration.

Hunt glanced across the cab to find him scowling at his cell phone. "Aw, is your fantasy football team fowling things up again?"

"No, there's a major pile-up on the freeway a few miles ahead. We should probably take a detour."

When he fell silent, Hunt nodded at his phone. "You're the one riding shotgun, so you're gonna have to navigate us around it."

His father squinted at his phone screen and rattled off a few directions.

Hunt's brows rose. "You sure the downtown area is our best bet?" He imagined it would be quicker to take the outer belt.

"Hey!" His father threw up his hands in mock

defense. "I thought you delegated the navigating to me."

"Downtown it is." Hunt hunched his shoulders over the steering wheel, though he could think of a good two to three more sensible routes to take. Then again, he was the guy who'd been gone for ten years. What did he really know about the streets of Dallas these days?

Very little, apparently, from the roadblock he approached a few minutes later.

"I can't catch a break today," he muttered, feathering his brakes and pulling abreast of the patrol car idling in front of the blockade.

A man in a blue uniform stepped from the vehicle and approached Hunt's rolled-down window. "Welcome home, Staff Sergeant Ryker!"

Hunt stared in puzzlement at the blonde and freckled deputy. "Do I know you, officer?"

"Nope." The man's face relaxed into a grin. "I recognized you from all the posters."

"What posters?"

He chuckled as he ducked his head to peer inside the truck cab. "Oh, hey, Mr. Ryker! Good to see you, too."

Hunt's father gave the young deputy a two-fingered salute.

Hunt shot a suspicious look at him. "What's going on?"

"I promised your mother I wouldn't spoil the

surprise, so please don't start asking a bunch of questions."

The deputy glanced curiously between the two of them. "How about you just follow me the rest of the way, Staff Sergeant?"

The rest of the way to where? Clenching his jaw, Hunt nodded, though discomfort twisted his gut. All he'd wanted was a quiet, uneventful trip home, but it sounded like his mother had other ideas. For the life of him, he couldn't imagine what in the world she'd planned that required a blockade and a police escort.

As he followed the trooper's vehicle down the sunny highway, he could make out a cluster of yet more vehicles in the distance. They weren't a typical collection of cars and trucks, either. As he drove closer, Hunt could see that they were decorated in a festive hodgepodge of red, white, and blue. In addition to all the ribbons and streamers, there were flags waving and life-sized posters of him on display.

You have got to be kidding me! There were convertible sports cars, trucks pulling floats, and two television crew vans. Additionally, there was a high school band present, marching in place while beating on a series of drums.

"You're killing me, Dad," he muttered. "Absolutely killing me!"

"Whoa! Don't take it out on the messenger. This was all your mom's idea," his father informed him with a wry grin. "All I did was stretch the truth a bit.

This is the real reason she couldn't make it to Fort Sam Houston today."

Because she was planning a blasted parade? Hunt parked where he was directed and stepped from his truck amidst a wild round of applause, whistles, and cheers.

He quickly lost sight of his father as he was hustled to the front of the parade. There he was waved to an elaborately decorated float emblazoned with the letters U.S.O.

A gorgeous brunette in a white sundress smiled a greeting to him from a platform where she was waving at the crowd. A very familiar-looking brunette, though they'd never met face-to-face before now.

"Dallas?" His jaw dropped in surprise. "Dallas Hill?" Yep, he'd recognize those fascinating blue eyes and fine-boned features anywhere. She was the hometown actress who'd made it all the way to the big screen by starring in a blockbuster movie called A Girl With A Badge. On set, she played the role of a police officer fresh from the academy, who was sent to serve in a K9 unit. Ultimately — at least in her fictional world — she'd tracked down a pair of kidnapped children in time to save them. She might as well have been a real hero, though, from the way her rabid following of fans worshipped her. Funny how heroes were made sometimes. Besides being a public icon, she was hot

— smoking firebrand hot — both on and off the screen.

"The one and only Dallas Hill," she returned cheerfully, beckoning him to mount the stairs and join her at the top of the float, "though I've already been accused twice today of not being the real Dallas." She flipped back a handful of her long, dark hair and eyed him laughingly.

He arched his brows at her as he ascended the short flight of stairs, remaining on the second-to-last rung to bring them eye level. "Okay, I'll bite. Who do your accusers think you are?"

"One of my stunt doubles."

"Really?" He used her words as an excuse to swiftly scan her slender, athletic frame. *Whew!* Hot didn't even begin to describe her. She was stunning, the take-your-breath-away kind of stunning — all willowy and perfect. Glad that she didn't know the way her nearness was making his heart pound, he inquired, "How many doubles do you have?"

"Three," she confessed with a smile. "A Nascar driver for the police chases, a champion rock climber for scaling the city buildings, and a female boxer for the fights." She wrinkled her nose ruefully at him. "One of them got banged up pretty good on set the other night. They're the real heroes in the movie, not me."

"Huh. I doubt all your fans clamoring for a second movie would agree." He liked her humble attitude. It was both unexpected and refreshing coming from a celebrity. He'd met his fair share of them during backstage passes at USO shows while deployed, and humble usually wasn't at the top of their list of attributes.

Her smile slipped. "There's not going to be a second movie." She turned away from him and resumed waving at the crowd.

"Really? Why's that?" Thoroughly intrigued, Hunt limped up the final stair and joined her at the rail. The cheering intensified as he took his place beside her.

"This is the part where you wave and pretend like you want to be here," she informed him through wide, smiling lips.

Man, I hate this! He mechanically held up his hand and was dismayed when the crowd started to chant. "Welcome home! Welcome home! Welcome home!"

"I'm told this was all my mother's idea," he grumbled, wanting Dallas to know this was not how he'd planned to spend his afternoon. "I really wish she hadn't gone to all this trouble."

"She probably had a lot of requests to make this happen. Our town genuinely appreciates your service, soldier." She shot him an admiring glance. "They know they're in the presence of an honest-to-gosh hero."

"I'm no hero!" He was aghast to see children in

the crowd who were dressed up like soldiers. Little did they understand how un-glamorous a life it actually was to serve in the United States Armed Forces. "I'm just a regular guy who got caught in an ambush and lived to talk about it."

"And risked your life to save your buddy, which is kind of the definition of a hero," she reminded. "Everyone knows they don't hand out Purple Hearts to just anyone. So paste on your biggest smile and try to pretend like you're enjoying yourself."

If only it were that easy! Feeling lightheaded, Hunt leaned forward to grip the railing with both hands, staring out at the sea of faces. They deserved to know the truth, didn't they? That there was a battle still waging over in Afghanistan that he never got to finish fighting. That there were soldiers missing, families grieving, and not everyone was going to get to come home in the end.

"Maybe this will help take your mind off the worst of it," Dallas sighed at his elbow. "Let's give this crowd what they really came for, shall we?"

Whatever that may be... Still staring blindly at the crowd, Hunt felt her lift one of his hands to step between him and the rail. Then she stood on her tiptoes to press her lips to his.

CHAPTER 2: CELEBRITY STUNT

DALLAS

Dallas could hear the crush of parade attendees shrieking their approval as she planted a kiss on their hometown hero. A tiny sliver of guilt worked its way through her at the thought that her actions might be perceived as a shameless grab for publicity. Through her closed lids, she could still see the flash of cameras. Yeah, her ratings were going to go through the roof when the candid photographs of her pressed up against Hunt Ryker's Purple Heart flooded across social media. According to her agent, moments like these were branding in its purest form.

Seconds later, product branding was the last thing on her mind as Hunt's hard mouth softened and moved over hers — questing, sampling, and cherishing. She sensed a surprising amount of anger and frustration in him, a dozen other emotions she couldn't define, and undeniable male attraction. By the time he lifted his head, she could no longer remember the time, their location, or the universe they were standing in.

There was only Hunt. As she stared up at him in astonishment, he muttered, "Sorry. I haven't kissed a girl in over two years."

"Two years?" she squeaked. *Um, wow!* No wonder his kiss had packed such an emotional wallop. She'd only intended for it to be a quick and sweet photo op, but he'd given her a lot more than she'd bargained for.

"Yeah." He didn't seem to realize he still had one arm hooked around her waist. "Guess I'm more out of practice than I realized."

She gave a breathy chuckle, tipping her head against his shoulder while trying to catch her breath. *Gosh!* The guy was seriously built. He practically radiated strength. It was enough to make her head spin.

"Is that what you think? Then again, what do I know?" She scrambled for a light and teasing comeback, since he seemed genuinely distressed about her reaction to his kiss. "I mainly neck on stage." She waved offhandedly. "You know, the super choreographed stuff that's part of the job."

Some of the tension left his tall frame. "Dare I ask where our kiss ranked in the realm of screenworthy kisses?"

Regaining her composure enough to raise her

head from his shoulder, she murmured, "Trust me, you have nothing to worry about in that department."

Their audience transitioned from a riot of clapping and wolf-whistling to chanting, "USA! USA! USA!"

Hunt seemed to be tuning them out, though she managed to raise her hand and start waving again.

"No, seriously." He didn't sound ready to let the topic go just yet, and his grin was doing crazy things to her heart as he prodded, "On a scale of one to ten, where did our kiss rank?"

She waved a finger beneath his nose. "Now you're just fishing."

His slate-gray gaze sparkled with mischief. "As energetically as a crawfish trapper with a net full of herring bait."

"Fine." She chuckled, finding his quick-whip humor irresistible. "On a scale of one to ten, it was a fifty."

His squared-off, sun-burnished features were infused with a delicious shade of red. "Now you're just messing with me."

"Maybe a little," she admitted, chuckling, "but our kiss wasn't bad." More like mind-blowing. Her brain was still reeling over the fact that she was the first girl he'd kissed in over two years.

"Ouch!" His hand flew to his chest as he pretended to be wounded. "Guess making the not-bad column is better than landing in the bad column."

"Wave, soldier," she commanded with a smile

He dutifully raised his hand again. To her disappointment, however, he dropped his arm from her waist when he did so.

At least he didn't seem in any hurry to step away and put any distance between them. They continued to wave, side-by-side, at their audience, as the float slowly crawled its way down the crowded city streets. Cars were jammed in all the available parking spots, with their owners sitting on both bumpers and hoods. Other spectators pressed close behind them — a good ten to fifteen layers of humanity spilling all the way back to the store-front buildings.

The shop windows were plastered with red, white, and blue Welcome Home signs. Most were addressed to Hunt. Some bore photos of him in uniform. A few displayed Purple Heart medals. One bold store owner even had a life-sized cardboard cutout of him displayed next to their front entrance.

"How did so many people find out about this parade?" he grumbled. "It's not as if my exit date from the Marines was set in stone."

Dallas bit back a chuckle at his disgruntled tone. "A lot of people helped spread the word. VFW halls, the local Daughters of the American Revolution chapter, the Boys Scouts and Girl Scouts, a few news stations, and your own mother, of course. She's a force to be reckoned with." She shook her head. The woman had seriously mobilized every ladies auxiliary, book club, and tea group in the city to welcome her son home. It was a truly impressive accomplishment.

"That she is." He leaned forward to rest his forearms on the railing. With the way his face had whitened beneath his tan, she could only assume he was in some sort of pain.

"Are you okay?" she asked quickly. "We can sit down, if you want."

"Nah, I'm good," he muttered, flexing his left leg a few times.

"Well, we need to keep waving." Because of how pale he continued to look, she wriggled her way beneath one of his arms once again. "How about I stay right here?" Keeping an arm around his middle and her legs firmly locked against the floor of the float, she waved frenziedly with the other hand.

"I'm sorry," he bit out. His grimace as he straightened told her he was in actual pain.

"For what?" she asked lightly, wishing there was something more she could do for him.

"For the fact that you're stuck with a broken-down soldier on this parade, instead of a guy who can stand a full hour on his own two feet."

"Whatever," she snorted. "I'm honored to be here."

"Right."

"It's true." She squinted through the sun up at him, hating the disbelief in his voice. "Why are you so angry at the world, anyway?"

His gaze turned flinty. "I'm not angry at anybody in particular. I'm just angry."

"Fair enough. Why?" Maybe it was poor manners on her part to keep pushing him, but at least her questions seemed to be bringing some of the color back to his face.

He shrugged and dragged in a deep breath. "Because I didn't get to finish what I started. The fight is over for me, but my buddies are still back there in the desert, risking their lives. And I'm not there to help."

"I'm sorry," she murmured. "I can't exactly stand here and claim to understand what you're going through, but—"

"In your world, it would probably feel like being yanked out of a movie at the halfway point." He jerkily waved a hand. "One where you never get to finish filming the scene. Or a book that ends in the middle and you never get to find out who wins — the good guys or the bad guys."

"That *would* be tough," she murmured regretfully.

"You have no idea."

"But I would like to," she confessed softly,

venturing another glance up at him from beneath her lashes.

He looked troubled. "Please assure me that doesn't mean you're thinking about enlisting in the military."

She scowled. "I'm not sure why you think that would be such a bad idea, but no. My path is taking me in a different direction." She'd just received her acceptance letter to the police academy and was trying to work up the courage to break the news to her agent. He was going to flip out in a thousand different ways when he realized how serious she was about leaving her acting career behind.

Hunt nodded curtly. "I think I speak for the rest of the world when I say I hope your path involves filming a sequel to A Girl With A Badge."

Disappointment sliced through her. "Hmm. I figured you, of all people, would understand. Guess I was wrong." So much for their one amazing kiss. He was just another guy who saw just a pretty face when he looked at her.

"Understand what?" He arched one of his thick, dark eyebrows at her in a way that made her wish she could film a movie with *him* before she exited the stage.

Right. She'd never gotten around to explaining herself. "I'm leaving show business to attend the police academy."

"I see." His hard mouth twitched at the corners.

"A girl with a fake badge who decided she wants to turn it into a real one, eh?"

"As a matter of fact, yes." She lifted her chin. "Go ahead. Laugh. You wouldn't be the first."

"I don't feel like laughing."

She swallowed the rush of hope his words gave her, knowing he was probably only being nice. "Or take a pot shot at how foolish an actress like me is for thinking that solving real crime will be all cozy cut-and-dry like it is on screen."

He grunted. "So long as it's not what *you* think."

"Of course not!"

"Then no pot shots are necessary," he retorted, reaching over to give a strand of her hair a light tug.

"Well, you didn't seem all that excited about the notion of an actress enlisting in the military, so I wasn't sure what you would think of an actress joining the police force."

He glanced away from her. "Though it's none of my business, I'm not all that excited about any scenario where you end up injured or worse."

"It's sweet of you to say that." She hugged him a little tighter.

"I have a few redeeming qualities," he retorted dryly. "Not many, so don't get your hopes up."

She bit her lower lip, wondering if it his way of saying their one kiss was going nowhere. It was way too bad, because she liked what she saw in Staff

Sergeant Hunt Ryker. A lot. Enough to want to see him again.

"So what's next for you?" she heard herself asking, hoping to keep their conversation going a little longer.

"I have no idea." He shifted his weight from one foot to the next, looking strained...and still in pain, a fact that tugged at her heart strings. "Got a friend at the firehouse trying to talk me into applying for a job. Plus, I have some contacts at the Texas Hotline Training Center, who seem to think I might be a good fit there in one of their instructor positions."

No way! She'd fully planned on applying for one of their hard-to-get student slots after she graduated from the police academy. What were the odds of her ending up in the same search and rescue program as the hunky wounded vet? *Good gracious!* The thought rendered her lightheaded — in a good way, though. "Snagging one of their certifications is high on my to-do list." Once she earned a real badge plus her credentials in search and rescue (SAR) operations, she planned to specialize in tracking down missing people. Knowing her career as an actress had sparked her interest in that line of work, she braced herself for a bit of well-deserved ribbing.

Hunt didn't so much as crack a smile. He nodded, his expression unreadable. "It would be cool if we ended up there together."

"It totally would." She tried to tamp down on her

disappointment at the lack of inflection in his voice. He certainly didn't sound like a guy about to ask a girl on a date. *Oh, well.*

Sometime the stars simply weren't aligned for romance — not even for a girl who'd worked as hard as she had to finagle a ride on the USO float with the city's biggest hometown hero. At least, she'd managed to stage a camera-worthy kiss that would be plastered all over social media before nightfall. Her agent would be thrilled. Still, it was way too bad this was going to be the beginning and end of her brief encounter with Hunt Ryker.

Regardless, she was pretty sure it was going to be a long time — a *very* long time — before she got their kiss out of her head.

CHAPTER 3: THE ACADEMY

HUNT

Nine months later

Hunt drove his truck and U-Haul trailer through the entrance gates of the Texas Hotline Training Center, amazed all over again at what he was seeing on the other side of the fence. Anyone driving by the school could see the three-story stacked stone fortress of a home office from the highway and assume whatever they wanted about the rigor of the program. But up close like this, it was so much more than a school. It was a mini city in its own right, set in the heart of Texas amidst a trio of lakes where the SAR instructors conducted their water rescue training.

The mountains in the distance were used for avalanche training during the winter months and other high-altitude rescues year-round. As Hunt drove around the central building that housed the indoor classrooms and main auditorium, he passed the kennel where the K9-certified dogs were boarded.

As if on cue, his black cocker spaniel, PoPo, gave a yip of excitement from his cage resting on the passenger seat. PoPo had been a gift from Hunt's parents upon his return home. Since the service dog he'd trained and deployed with had remained with his Marine unit, they figured he would want a dog of his own.

They'd been right. While serving with the military police, Hunt couldn't have imagined doing the challenging work they were tasked with — tracking down and routing out enemy combatants — without the assistance of his K9 partner. Civilian life was proving to be no different.

In an attempt to remain in town near his family, he'd tried his hand at firefighting. In the end, though, handling service dogs had become so much a part of who he was that he'd ultimately decided to get back to doing it full time. What he wasn't a hundred percent sure about was if he was meant to do it from the role of an instructor. Before now, he'd always served on the front lines. Did he have what it took to train others to deploy to the front lines while he remained in the safety of the sidelines? Only time would tell.

He reached over to rest a hand on PoPo's cage. "This is going to be our new home, buddy." For a

THE SECRET BABY RESCUE   35

while, anyway. At least until he figured out if he was capable of making a difference in the world from the sidelines.

His friend and fellow Marine, Axel Hammerstone, had been twisting his arm for months about applying for a position at the training center. His wife worked here and loved it. Hunt's head was still spinning over how quickly he'd received a job offer from the training center's officials after his interview. Apparently, serving ten years as a K9 certified military police in the Marine Corps was the perfect resume in their book. He sincerely hoped he lived up to their expectations in the coming weeks.

It had been nine months since his discharge from the hospital. Though he still walked with a bit of a limp, it wasn't so bad these days. Thanks to a few very skilled surgeons at the burn center in San Antonio, the wounds on his lower back and legs were healing nicely. He'd endured more than a dozen skin grafts beneath their wizardly hands, and not one of them looked too shabby unless a person was standing really close.

A bump in the road jostled another bark out of PoPo.

"Sorry, buddy." Hunt slowed his truck to a crawl as they approached a series of pot holes in the pavement. A line of orange cones directed him away from the holes, forcing him to swing into the other lane to get around them. It was a two-lane road, surrounded by grassy training fields on both sides. Fortunately, there were no oncoming drivers in the other lane.

A sharp honk from behind had him squinting into his rearview mirror. A man in a black pickup flung an arm out his window and waved, as if trying to get him to pull over.

Oka-a-ay. Hunt finished driving around the orange cones, then pulled to the curb and idled his motor.

The black pickup pulled alongside him and its driver leaned across his cab to shout, "Hey, there! You must be Staff Sergeant Ryker." He was a bulldog of a man with a no-nonsense expression, a shaved head, and an interesting-looking tattoo riding behind one ear when he lifted his ball cap. No, on second guess, it was probably a birth mark. An interesting bluish-black one that covered a good six inches of skin, roughly the shape of Australia.

"I am." Hunt inclined his head in acknowledgement, curious about who the guy was.

"Figured that, since I didn't recognize your truck. Plus, the U-Haul sorta advertised the fact that you're moving in. I'm Jug Dawson, by the way."

Ah. My new boss. Though Hunt had never met the guy, he could recite his credentials like the back of his hand. Officer Jug Dawson was something of a legend at the training center. He'd started off his illustrious career in the Special Forces, then did a five-year stint with the Dallas PD, and eventually had taken on the responsibility of the Missing Persons Division chair at the prestigious Texas Hotline Training Center. He also served as the lead instructor of the division.

Hunt inclined his head again. "Nice to finally meet you, Officer Dawson."

"Likewise." The instructor's wide mouth turned down at the corners. "Sorry I was on vacay while you were interviewing, but don't worry. I was on video cam during your interview."

"Oh?" Hunt frowned. "You were?" He recalled someone mentioning the interview was being recorded, but he didn't recall any mention of the absent Officer Dawson listening in and observing it.

"Yep." The man grinned. "Right down to the way you got all uncomfortable over the question about where you saw yourself five years from now — professionally speaking."

Great. So you figured out I'm probably only going to be a short-termer here at the training center. Knowing that getting off on the wrong foot with one's new boss could spell quick and certain disaster for him, Hunt wisely kept his silence.

"Relax, Staff Sergeant." Jug Dawson smirked. "The fact that you're not all hopped up over your new title and position is one of the biggest reasons I recommended they hire you."

"You did?" Hunt tensed, wondering what the catch was. He couldn't think of many good reasons why someone would hire him for a job he wasn't overly enthusiastic about filling.

"Yep. Some of the lesser experienced candidates were a little too gaga over the prestige of the place for my tastes. Figured if I could convince a soldier with your background to actually *want* to serve in a training capacity, I'd be stacking my team with the right kind of folks."

Hunt's jaw dropped. "I'm honored that you feel that way, sir."

"Yeah, well, I'm not counting my chickens yet, Staff Sergeant. I can tell I have my work cut out with you."

Hunt wasn't quite sure how to respond to that. Fortunately, PoPo chose that moment to insert himself into the conversation with an excited yip.

Officer Dawson looked amused. "I take it that small but mighty beast is your service dog?"

"Yes, sir. We've been training together for a little over eight months now."

"He's a cute little squirt."

Hunt pretended to be horrified as he faced his dog. "It's alright, PoPo. The officer didn't mean that how it sounded." Then he shook his head in mock warning at his boss. "He may look like a house pet, but inside his head, he's ten feet tall with blood dripping from his fangs."

"Duly noted." Jug Dawson guffawed and clapped his ball cap back on his head. "Well, good luck on dodging the potholes. We had a late snow that didn't do our roads any favors. Our repair crew is still working to get caught up."

Hunt gave him a thumbs up signal.

"Oh, and I'd appreciate seeing you at our three o'clock class this afternoon."

You would? Hunt glanced down at his watch to discover it was already ten minutes 'til noon.

"I know that doesn't leave you much time to get settled in, but our latest crop of recruits started last week. It's probably best to get the introductions behind us today, so you can hit the ground running in the morning."

"No problem, sir. I'll be there."

"Good, and bring your dog. May as well introduce all the stars on our cast at one time."

"Yes, sir." He'd been hoping to spend the afternoon getting moved in, so he could turn in the rented U-Haul a day early. *Oh, well.* Life in the Marines had taught him not to question orders, no matter how inconvenient they were. He was well accustomed to rolling with the punches.

PoPo's answering yip made it sound like he was in perfect agreement with starting work right away.

"Alright, then. See you in a few." Officer Dawson shot them a quick salute and gunned his motor to head on down the road.

Staring with interest after the man, Hunt couldn't help noticing the Purple Heart on his mud-splattered license plate. Another wounded vet, eh? Looked like he was going to be in good company at the training center.

He pulled back into his lane and continued driving at a super slow pace so he could gawk at his surroundings. He drove by the wreckage of an airplane, the rubble of several burned-out buildings, and a football-sized field overgrown with weeds. He could only assume they were some the areas staged for simulated training exercises.

Next were the dormitories — one for the male trainees and one for the female trainees, according to the full-color brochure they'd sent him home with after his interview. Down the street from the dorms was a row of townhouses for permanent staff members like him. Beyond the townhouses were some smaller, cozy-looking cabins.

Hunt crawled past the row of tan stucco townhouses, looking for the one that matched the number on the key he'd been given. And there it was, three doors down on the right — 101C. Backing his U-Haul trailer into the driveway, he mashed the button on the keyring remote and was pleased to see that the garage door had been programmed correctly.

He leaped down and jogged around to the passenger door to let out PoPo. The dog quickly snuffled his way to the garage, stopping to sniff first at a pebble and secondly at a grass spider that was skedaddling as fast as he could across the concrete toward the front yard.

Traversing the garage to open the door leading inside, Hunt found himself in a laundry room. It contained a stackable washer and dryer on one side and a mudroom bench on the other side. Hooks for hanging jackets and other gear were mounted on the wall above it.

Hunt stepped past a sliding door to the kitchen. It boasted an open layout and a wide bar that overlooked the living room. The only door off the living area led to his master bedroom and bathroom. A sliding glass door in the dining area beside the kitchen led to a tiny patio enclosed by a wooden railing. The *piece de résistance* was the fact that it overlooked an enormous lake.

Nice! He gave a low whistle. It was the perfect space for a single guy — exactly what he needed to house his bachelor collection of video games and dial-up weights, as well as his workout bench and tower.

PoPo, who had followed him inside, quickly made his rounds, exploring and sniffing his way through every corner of every room.

"What do you think, buddy? Do you like it here?" Since PoPo was still too busy exploring to answer, Hunt selected a corner of the kitchen near the sliding glass door to set out the dog's water and food bowls.

PoPo happily came to inspect his corner of the kitchen and remained long enough to lap up some water from his bowl.

Hunt carried in his suitcases next and dumped them inside his bedroom, taking a quick detour to the adjoining bathroom to toss his toiletry bag on the vanity. Returning to his bedroom, he unpacked and hung up his new uniforms first.

Next, he hauled in his king-sized bed from the U-Haul one piece at a time. The mattresses were the toughest thing to carry without any assistance. They weren't heavy; they were just bulky. Fortunately, Hunt's townhouse was one-story and he'd rented a furniture dolly, so it was mostly a matter of rolling and steering the parts of the bed around corners.

All he had the time to do was assemble it. He'd have to wait until after class to throw on his sheets and blankets. *Not a bad start.* He'd made good use of the limited block of time and was at least partially moved in. Since he'd worked up a sweat while hauling in furniture, he took a quick shower before changing into one of his new uniforms.

Staring at it in the mirror gave him a strange feeling. The solid black fabric was a far cry from his Marine camouflage. The uniform consisted of a cargo shirt and trousers, an official training center name badge with the words Instructor Ryker emblazoned across it, and black combat boots. Accustomed to military neatness, he'd taken the time to iron it, so there were crisp creases in his shirt sleeves and the outer edge of his trousers. It probably wasn't required, but old habits died hard. Smirking at his meticulous appearance, he pressed on his black ball cap, which also bore the Texas Hotline Training Center (THTC) logo, and pivoted away from the mirror.

Giving a sharp whistle that brought PoPo running, he buckled the dog into his K9 tactical vest and stuffed his leash inside the pocket of his trousers. Dressing PoPo in his gear was the dog's signal that they were about to report to duty. He was so excited that he ran a few circles around the empty living room, barking.

"Atta boy. Mount up," Hunt ordered briskly.

Well aware that this was a command to return to his cage in the truck, PoPo obediently headed for the door leading to the garage.

Hunt latched him into his cage in the passenger seat and rewarded his good behavior with one of his favorite milk-bones. Then he finished backing the U-Haul trailer the rest of the way into the garage and unhitched it. He lowered the garage door with his remote control as he drove off.

A text from Jug Dawson while he was setting up his bed indicated they would be meeting at the staging area behind the auditorium. Apparently, this was where they would normally gather equipment and load vehicles for the occasional calls the training center received to help handle emergencies in neighboring towns. Hunt had been told during his interview that not all the small towns nearby were equipped with luxuries like bomb squads and certified search and rescue teams, so it was a win-win for everyone. The towns received high-quality assistance for specialized situations, while the training center's students got to apply their newly acquired skills during these real-life crises.

Hunt had no idea how often these events occurred. He was just glad to hear there was a chance he'd be called to handle a real emergency now and then. Hopefully, that meant he'd get a little front line action, after all.

He parked at the curb and let PoPo out, giving him a sharp command to sit while he attached the dog's leash. "Good boy." He whistled to get him moving again. "Let's go meet our new team, PoPo."

The dog's name had started off as something of a joke by Hunt's mother, Hallie Ryker, who'd served her entire adult life as a 911 call operator in Dallas. When Hunt was growing up, she'd warned him countless times that he'd better behave or the "PoPo would come get him." Apparently, she'd made the same threat a few times to the frisky one-year-old pup before Hunt's arrival home. He'd come running every time, so the name had stuck.

A brisk March breeze whipped at the sturdy fabric of Hunt's black cargo uniform as he jogged across the near-empty parking lot. It made him glad he'd opted to wear one of his dry-wick compression shirts underneath. Despite his ever-present limp, it also felt good to work out the rest of the stiffness from his drive to the training center. He'd always enjoyed running and the endorphins it inevitably kicked up.

Officer Dawson was already present, along with all six of his trainees — four men and two women. They were standing in a semi-circle, while he demonstrated the use of a bite sleeve, a thickly padded arm covering that was often used in dog training exercises.

"Atten-shun!" Jug Dawson snapped out the order as Hunt drew abreast of their small huddle.

All six trainees snapped to the soldierly position of attention with their legs together and their arms hanging at their sides.

"Right on time." The lead instructor nodded his approval at Hunt. "I'm pleased to welcome your new instructor, Staff Sergeant Hunt Ryker." He gestured at Hunt. "As you can tell, we're ramping up for a session with the bite sleeves in the morning. Feel free to take the floor and add in your ten cents."

Hunt nodded. "Thank you, Officer Dawson. At ease, trainees." He swiftly perused the six students to get some idea of what he was dealing with, age-wise and experience-wise.

The first student was a tanned and wiry Hispanic man with the name Sanchez on his name badge. Next was a tall, willowy blonde woman with the last name of Miller. Beside her was a smirking, hovering jokester named Haliburton, who immediately set Hunt's teeth on edge. He knew the guy's type all too well — a nauseatingly macho jerk who took few things seriously other than his hallowed gym routine, from the looks of his well-sculpted shoulders and biceps. Fortunately, his attitude was nothing that a little serious training couldn't cure.

Standing beside the jokester were two red-headed, freckled men, Evans and Evans, who faces and name badges were mirror images of each other. *Twins?* Hunt shot a curious look at his lead instructor, who merely shrugged. The last woman in the group turned out to be an all-too-familiar face — one who served a sharp, swift punch of remembrance to Hunt's gut.

No way! Dallas Hill was actually one of his students! What were the odds of that?

He forced his gaze to rove blandly over her as he strove to ignore the memory of their kiss. The way her expressive blue eyes darkened with awareness wasn't helping, though. Neither was the way she was nervously biting her lush lower lip.

Just seeing her again was a reminder that he was the world's biggest idiot for not picking up the phone and calling her to ask her out on a date. There had been instant chemistry between them during their first encounter. Chemistry he'd first tried to convince himself that he'd imagined. Chemistry he'd later told himself he had no right to pursue, considering he was jobless at the time and uncertain about what came next. Chemistry he was feeling all over again right now. Big-time!

A snicker made Hunt's head spin back toward the jokester. "Did I say something funny, Trainee Haliburton?"

"No, sir. I, er, was just thinking that your dog looks cute." His smirk clearly indicated that he thought a Marine with a cocker spaniel for a search and rescue dog was something worthy of scoffing at.

Hunt shrugged. "Looks can be deceiving. PoPo is capable of taking down a person more than ten times his size and weight." Probably more like twenty times his size and weight, but Hunt didn't mind saving that surprise for later.

While the Ken doll of a student chuckled in derision, PoPo growled menacingly in the back of his throat.

Quickly losing patience with the guy, Hunt turned to Officer Dawson. "Mind if I get us started on the live part of our training, sir?" He had every intention of wiping the mocking look off the student's face.

"Not at all, Instructor Ryker." Eyes twinkling, the stocky lead instructor divested himself of the bite sleeve and tossed it in Hunt's direction. In one swift movement, Hunt caught it and sent it zinging onward in Haliburton's direction.

The trainee jolted in surprise, but managed to catch it after stumbling back a step.

"You're up, Haliburton," Hunt announced, "that is, if you're ready to take your best shot at warding off an attack from a killer cocker spaniel."

"You're on, sir." The cocky trainee actually grinned in anticipation.

Poor sap! "Anyone else who'd like a turn with the bite sleeve this afternoon will get their chance next. Until then, watch and learn." Hunt waved their group off the patch of pavement they were standing on to the dry, grassy clearing adjacent to the parking lot. Then he moved Haliburton's classmates back a good additional ten feet or so from the bite sleeve before giving PoPo his first command.

To throw off Haliburton, Hunt put the agile canine through his paces first. He removed the dog's favorite reward from the backpack on his shoulder, a miniature orange basketball.

"Aww…" the tall blonde student cooed in a voice that most women reserved for babies or small children.

PoPo actually loved to be talked to in that tone of voice, but Hunt didn't want to give Haliburton the satisfaction of learning that just yet. Instead, he scowled at the woman, and she lapsed into silence as he threw the ball. PoPo joyfully pounced on it, looking every bit like an adorable house pet to those gathered around him. It was a mistaken assumption that Hunt was about to correct.

As the dog trotted past Haliburton, Hunt snapped out the next command. "Attack!"

PoPo spat out the ball and moved so fast that he was nothing more than a dark blur. He sailed through the air like a coiled spring, sank his teeth into the bite sleeve, and gave a vicious yank that forced Haliburton to dance sideways to keep his footing. Before he could fully right himself, the cocker spaniel kicked his hind legs out at the unwitting fellow's knees and used the movement as leverage to give another yank on the bite sleeve, this time in the opposite direction.

Not having expected the unusual maneuver from such an innocent looking animal, Haliburton's legs shot out from underneath him, making him lose his balance and tumble to the ground.

PoPo was immediately on top of him, snapping and growling up a storm.

Hunt called off his dog, who promptly trotted over to reclaim his discarded orange ball. He carried it back to Hunt, his black and white tail wagging victoriously.

Haliburton's shocked classmates started to clap as if it was a wrestling match and the dog had won.

"He cheated," Haliburton blustered, scrambling to his feet and furiously dusting the dirt stains from his black trousers. "How was I supposed to know your furry little pet was demonically possessed? Give me another shot. I'm ready now."

Hunt gave him an innocent look. "The element of surprise is kinda the whole idea, trainee." Feeling no small amount of satisfaction over the fact that Dallas had gotten to witness how thoroughly he'd put her cocky classmate in his place, Hunt returned his gaze to the group at large. "Your dogs are like loaded weapons. By the end of this course, you'll know when, why, and how to properly fire them at your targets."

He glanced around the small, grinning group. None of them seemed too bothered by Haliburton's crabbing. "Now that you've seen one of PoPo's secret maneuvers, would anyone else like the opportunity to ward off an attack from him? Otherwise, Haliburton is up for round two."

Five hands shot up. The bite sleeve was passed down the line. One by one, PoPo sent them all sprawling to the ground — including Haliburton on his second attempt at defending himself.

"He's amazing," Dallas breathed, as she took her turn dusting off her clothing and retrieving her cap that had gotten knocked off.

Hunt privately hoped she hadn't gotten too bruised or scratched up during her tumble. PoPo had shown no mercy with any of the trainees. *Little show-off!*

"He might be small, but I can totally picture him stopping an assault or foiling a kidnapping." She shook her head at the dog in wonder.

"That's right, trainee." Hunt wagged his finger at the group of students. "And all six of you are going to train your dogs to do exactly that tomorrow."

"Bright and early, new recruits. Bright and early." Officer Dawson, who'd stepped away to take a phone call, rejoined their group with the bouncing grace of a boxer re-entering the ring. "We'll form up at the training ring next to the kennels at five o'clock tomorrow morning for our first session. Then we'll disband for breakfast and reassemble at eight. You'll be bringing your dogs to both sessions. Are there any questions?"

"No, sir!" The trainees responded in a unified chorus.

"Class dismissed. Trainee Hill, I need you to stay an extra few minutes about a matter concerning your student file."

"Yes, sir." Looking puzzled, Dallas cast a furtive glance in Hunt's direction before facing the lead instructor. "Is there a problem with my file, sir?"

He waited until the other students had walked out of earshot. "I certainly hope not, Trainee Hill." He paused a beat before adding, "And Instructor Ryker." He waved his cell phone at them.

Hunt's heart sank to see a snapshot of him and Dallas displayed in full lip-lock. Most unfortunately, his new boss had managed to dig up the one kiss the two of them had shared during his welcome home parade nine months ago.

Are you kidding me? Hunt glared at Jug Dawson, wondering why the man hadn't given him the respect of a heads up before blasting him with the matter in front of a student. Not to mention it was really uncool of him to treat Dallas this way. At the moment, she might be a student at the search and rescue training center, but she was a respected actress and newly minted police officer in the outside world.

Glancing her way in concern, he noted that she'd turned a deep shade of scarlet beneath the visor of her cap. Then she turned so white that he feared she was about to pass out.

"I can explain, sir," he offered quickly, still furious at his boss for the callus way he was choosing to address the situation.

"I certainly hope so," the officer growled, "considering I'm giving you every chance to do so right now before the commander calls me into his office and roasts me over an open flame for besmirching the reputation of his precious training center."

Okay, maybe you have a point. Hunt waffled between the truth and some version of it and ultimately settled for the social media version of it. "It was one of those USO-sponsored parades where I kissed one of her stunt doubles. Not surprised you found out about it, since it was all over the news. The audience loved it, sir." He didn't volunteer the information that the actress, herself, had made it clear that same afternoon that she was *not*, in fact, one of her doubles.

"They weren't the only ones who loved it, from the looks of things, Staff Sergeant."

Hunt gave what he hoped was an offhand shrug. "Not going to lie, sir. It was the best welcome home gift ever."

Dallas made a faint moaning sound.

"A stunt double, you say?" Officer Collins glanced sharply back and forth between the two of them.

"Yes, sir. She had three of them. You're welcome to check up on the details with her agent. No doubt Trainee Hill can provide his contact information." Hunt was bluffing, of course. He had no idea what her agent was willing or not willing to say to back up his fib, should anyone decide to question the man about it.

Dallas nodded vehemently, and the color slowly returned to her cheeks. "I'm happy to provide that information, sir."

"I'm not sure that will be necessary. I'm more concerned about the two of you assuring me that you can keep things professional here during our training."

"Absolutely, sir." Dallas flushed again.

"Not a problem on my end, sir," Hunt declared coolly. "If I didn't think I could act professionally around Trainee Hill, I would have voluntarily recused myself from the class the moment I laid eyes on her. To be truthful, I didn't even recognize her right away." That was another lie. He'd instantly known who she was. How could he forget? "I only met her one time, and that was nine months ago." That part was true, at least.

"Alright then. That's all I care about." Officer Dawson flipped off his cell phone and pocketed it. "If anyone asks for an explanation about the photo, I'll explain to them that Dallas Hill employed multiple stunt doubles."

"Thank you, sir." Hunt's gut told him that Officer Dawson wasn't a hundred percent sold on the explanation, but it appeared he was willing to let it go. For now.

Dallas sucked in a breath. "If I may add one more thing, sir."

Officer Dawson motioned for her to continue, looking curious.

Careful! Hunt groaned inwardly.

"I can't change the fact that I was an actress prior to becoming a police officer." Her embarrassment was gone. In its place was a coolly professional tone. "Not that I did anything I'm ashamed of, but I'm well aware of how many people out there don't consider starring in a romance movie to be a real job.

Despite that, I *did* succeed in gaining the respect of my classmates at the police academy, and I intend to do the same thing here at the training center."

Officer Dawson nodded in satisfaction. "I will personally guarantee you receive every opportunity to do so, Trainee Hill."

"Thank you, sir."

"It means no special treatment, though."

"I don't expect any, sir."

"And there will be no going easy on her, Staff Sergeant Ryker, just because she looks like a woman you've kissed before and enjoyed kissing, from the looks of that photo." Officer Dawson gave him a hard look.

"Understood, sir." Hunt's brain was already whirling with ideas for how to present an outward appearance of being tough and impartial on all matters concerning Dallas Hill — not only to his boss, but to her.

It wasn't going to be easy, though, considering how crystal clear his memories were about their first kiss, and how badly he already wanted to kiss her again.

CHAPTER 4: MENTAL TOUGHNESS

DALLAS

Dallas died a thousand deaths on the walk to her sporty red Jeep in the parking lot. *Mercy!* It was just her luck running into the one guy she'd been unable to forget during the past nine months, not that she'd tried very hard to forget him. Quite the opposite. Maybe she was crazy for obsessing over him the way she had, but the kiss they'd shared had gotten her through many tough training sessions at the police academy.

Most of her classmates had enjoyed the support of parents, siblings, spouses, and significant others to cheer them through the many challenges at the Dallas Police Academy. She had none of those people in her life — nothing to distract her from the rigors of her course work other than the memory of her heart-shaking first encounter with hometown hero Hunt Ryker.

And now she'd enjoyed her second encounter with him, which had been every bit as magical as the first — minus the kiss, of course. Over the past few months, she'd feared that her brain might have embellished her memories of him from the parade. If anything, however, her memories had fallen ridiculously short of the living, breathing, overpowering presence of the real Hunt Ryker.

He was taller than she remembered and broader. His skin tone was less pale and more swarthy, too, thanks to his Native American heritage. His father was a full-blooded Apache, a bona fide tribal member and everything.

In comparison, she was plain old melting-pot American, with a little of this and a little of that in her blood. And those were the highlights of her heritage. It was downhill from there.

She slammed her way into her Jeep and turned on the ignition. Revving the motor in a burst of anger, she exited the parking lot a little faster than necessary. Her mother was in jail on multiple counts of drug possession, and Dallas had no idea who her father was. She doubted her mother knew, either. Such was the life of a junkie. The best thing that had come from being raised in and out of foster care was her full-ride scholarship to a state university, one that had allowed her to join a theater club. Through a rather bizarre series of events, she'd been allowed to audition for A Girl With A Badge. Thus had begun her unlikely and rather miraculous rise to stardom.

She was still a woman with a dark and deplorable past, but at least she was a rich woman with a dark and deplorable past. A rich woman who now carried a police badge — one that had cost her no small amount of blood, sweat, and tears.

Longing to have someone to share the ups and downs of her day with, Dallas blinked back tears as she drove the short distance to the female student dormitory. For a split second, she debated placing one of those rare calls to her mother. Then again, what was the point? Despite the fact that her mother was in jail, she continued to find ways to get her hands on illegal drugs. For this reason, she was rarely sober. Which was probably how Dallas had ended up being named after the city where she was born.

Swallowing an elephant-sized dose of self pity, she parked outside the dormitory, leaped out of her Jeep, and jogged up the stairwell to her second-story room. Since she was going to miss her morning run, thanks to their bright and early training start time, it was probably best that she get in an extra run this evening. If nothing else, it would clear her brain from the tangle of emotions she'd been grappling with since laying eyes on Hunt Ryker again. With a little luck, the run would also make her tired enough to sleep tonight instead of lying awake thinking about him.

Changing into black yoga pants, a pale pink sweatshirt, and black sneakers, she made her way down the back stairwell and headed for the nearest lake path. All three lakes boasted trails for walking, running, and biking. She knew she was missing the dinner hour in the cafeteria, but she didn't care. She had a box of granola bars in her room to fall back on, if she got hungry enough.

Removing a stretchy band from her wrist, she reached up and used it to twist her hair into a hasty ponytail before breaking into a run. Her sneakers pounded the ground, making her revel in the sense of freedom it always gave her to have the wind rushing past her, whipping at her hair and clothing.

I didn't even recognize her right away. Hunt Ryker's words tumbled out of nowhere, nearly making her stumble. Was it true? Had their kiss been so unmemorable for him that he'd all but forgotten her while she was at the police academy?

A burst of anger made her hunker down into a sprint. She dashed a full fifty meters before slowing back to a jog. Breathing in her nose and out of her mouth, she forced her breathing back to a normal cadence.

It was one of those USO-sponsored parades where I kissed one of her stunt doubles. Dallas gave a moan of misery at the lie. He knew it was a lie, right? Surely, he hadn't talked himself into believing that falsehood after they'd parted! Then again, it had been the prevailing rumor of the day — that the real Dallas Hill was vacationing at a resort in Fiji while one of her doubles covered her latest marketing blitz for the movie.

She pondered the horrible possibility that Hunt Ryker might actually believe he'd kissed someone else, which would essentially amount to erasing their kiss altogether. Unable to bear the thought, she dug in her heels for a second sprint. Determined to run off all the negative energy poisoning her gut, she dashed several extra meters this time, pushing herself as hard as she could. Afterward, she had to jog with her hands clasped behind her head for a full minute to regain her breath.

Not going to lie, sir. It was the best welcome home gift ever. She blushed as she recalled the way Hunt's slate gaze had remained expressionless as he'd uttered those words. It was a good thing her face was already flushed from exertion, because her cheeks were positively flaming as she recalled his display of bland indifference.

Dallas canted her body forward for her third and final sprint. *Best welcome home gift ever. Best welcome home gift ever.* By the time she slowed her speed to a jog, she'd decided that those were the words she was going to hang on to. She wasn't going to spend the next several days beating herself up over whether Hunt Ryker had lied to protect her or himself. Or both of them. She was just going to keep pushing herself hard in training like she always did. And if her memories of their kiss continued to help motivate her, then so be it. They were her memories to handle however she wanted.

A movement at the patio railing of one of the instructor's townhomes captured her attention during her cool-down walk. She paused to stretch a few seconds, which gave her the chance to observe whoever it was from beneath her lashes.

Oh, gawsh! Of all people! It was Hunt Ryker leaning his forearms on the railing, much the same way he had during the parade. His leg had been killing him at the time, and it had been his way of shifting some of his weight away from it. Was it still hurting him after all this time?

Without thinking, she raised her head and stared right at him, taking a step in his direction. He caught her gaze and straightened to his full height, making her halt her approach.

No, he appeared to be fine, after all. A little embarrassed to be caught staring, she fluttered her hand in a quick wave and started walking again, much faster this time.

Instead of waving back, he pressed a hand to his heart.

She caught her breath at the gesture. It felt so deliberate, so intimate, as if he was trying to tell her something without using any words. Unfortunately, she didn't know what he meant. Was that his way of apologizing for their embarrassing encounter with Officer Dawson earlier? Worse yet, was he sorry they'd ever kissed in the first place — double or no double?

Please don't be sorry. Dallas found that she wasn't as tired as she originally thought she was, because she was able to squeak out one last sprint. This one took her nearly all the way back to the dormitory.

Fortunately, she'd utterly worn herself out and had no trouble falling asleep after her shower. She didn't wake up once during the night, and her alarm went off way too early the next morning.

The woman in the bed next to hers was already up, silently dressing in the dark.

"Missed you at dinner last night." Tracy Miller, the tall, beach blonde from class, glanced over her shoulder at the seven other sleeping women. Apparently, none of the other groups had received a five o'clock report time this morning from their instructors. *Lucky them!*

"I went for a run," Dallas whispered, yanking up her black cargo trousers and tucking in her uniform shirt.

"So I heard." Tracy shot her a sympathetic smile as she looped her shoulder-length blonde hair into a ponytail.

What's that supposed to mean? Dallas gave the woman a hard stare but didn't comment. Since her dark hair was so long, she took the time to weave it into two thick French braids. Her instincts told her that their upcoming training session was going to be brutal. She didn't want her hair in the way, making the training even more difficult. Also, if she took a little extra time with her hair, maybe Tracy would head on outside ahead of her. She wasn't in the mood to chitchat with a nosy classmate.

"Here. Let me." Tracy moved to stand behind her and took over braiding the right side. Though Dallas hadn't asked for her help, they finished in half the time it would've taken her to do both sides on her own.

"Thanks," she murmured gratefully, securing the two braids together behind her neck with a twisty tie. She mashed her hat on her head, and together they left the dormitory.

Tracy waited until they were outside before she spoke again. "Listen, I wasn't trying to butt into your business."

Really? Because it kinda sounded like you were. Dallas tensed, not sure how to respond.

"Okay, maybe I am butting in a little by what I'm about to say next. We should probably watch ourselves with Haliburton. He seems like a classic dirt bag, if you know what I mean."

Dallas gave a jerky nod, a little surprised by the woman's abrupt change of topics. "Seems like it, though he and I haven't had any problems, and I don't expect us to." She wasn't quite sure what her classmate was getting at.

"Our new instructor could become a problem for you. The same guy who supposedly kissed one of your doubles a few months ago." She gave Dallas a piercing look.

Dallas wrinkled her nose. "Great! I guess everybody knows about that by now." She didn't bother hiding her sarcasm. "It's really not that big of a deal."

"The big deal is that this same guy also took Haliburton down yesterday with a dang cocker spaniel," her classmate continued.

Dallas snorted out a laugh. "Yeah, that was pretty funny."

"It was," Tracy joined in the snickering, "to everyone but him." She sobered as they approached the kennels. "Just watch your step around him, okay?"

"I will. Thanks for the warning." Dallas gave her a two-fingered salute.

"Welcome." Tracy held up two fingers in answer, and they shared another chuckle before entering the kennels.

The dogs were barking frenziedly at the arrival of so many early, unexpected guests. Dallas and her five classmates quickly harnessed and leashed their service dogs and led them outside. Almost immediately, the barking inside the kennel abated.

Lady, Dallas's Doberman Pinscher, yanked on

her leash a few times, begging to be let loose for a run.

Dallas leaned down to give her a few firm, reassuring pets. "You'll get to run, girl. Soon. I promise." She felt a little guilty about not taking her dog on her run last night the way she normally did. At the time, she'd just needed to be alone.

To her surprise and disappointment, neither of their instructors were present, though it was obvious they'd shown up earlier and left. A tidy row of bite sleeve and bite suit silhouettes were hanging on the fence of the training ring, not too far from the entrance gate.

"That figures," Haliburton scoffed, jogging up to them with his dog. "Give us lackeys our marching orders while they continue drinking coffee and eating donuts."

Their huddle of classmates stepped inside the ring together.

Dallas swallowed a sigh at the venom in his voice. Choosing to ignore his snide jab at police officers in general, she unleashed her dog. Throwing a small, glow-in-the-dark ball, she whistled for Lady to go fetch it.

With a bark of glee, her dog dashed to the other side of the ring in pursuit of it.

The second time Dallas threw the ball, however, Haliburton hollered for his dog to go after it. His Rottweiler dashed with maddening energy across the ring and returned it, dripping with saliva, to Dallas. He'd utterly ruined her regular routine of putting her dog through her paces, and he knew it. A lesser trained dog than Lady might have started a fight over the disgustingly soaked toy.

Though Lady remained at Dallas's side, she didn't take the insult sitting down. She stood and growled in indignation as her owner removed the ball from the other dog's jaws. He growled back. Only when Dallas shot a questioning look at Haliburton did he laughingly order his dog to return to his side.

When he glanced around their circle of class-mates, however, he must have realized his mistake. All five of them were glaring in his direction. It was one thing to be a dirt bag. It was another thing entirely to mess with a fellow handler's dog during a training exercise. At the end of the day, their mission here at the Texas Hotline Training Center was about preparing their dogs to help save lives, not about chasing personal vendettas.

"What?" he snarled. "I was just messing around. Lighten up a little, will ya?"

When no one responded, he turned on his heel and whistled for his dog to follow. "That's it. I'm going back to bed."

In that same moment, two oversized pickup trucks rumbled into the parking lot. One was white, and one was black. Their headlights flashed across the training ring, drenching it with a blast of harsh light.

Dallas's heartbeat sped. It appeared that their instructors had returned.

"Going somewhere?" Instructor Dawson sang out to Haliburton's retreating figure as he swung his burly frame down from his truck.

"No, sir." Haliburton pivoted to face the ring. "Just taking a lap with my dog while we waited for you." His insolence about their lateness was unmistakable.

"No problem." Instructor Dawson's jaw tightened as he whipped off a pair of black gloves. "We'll wait while you finish." When Haliburton stood there staring, he waved his gloves at him. "Well, go on and run your lap."

Haliburton's face turned so red that Dallas instinctively stepped forward to defuse the situation. "Permission to join him, sir," she interjected breathlessly, hoping to preserve what little dignity her disgraced classmate had left.

The lead instructor raked her with his hard gaze, then nodded.

She clapped her hands. "Come on, Lady!" Her dog gave a yap of excitement and shot ahead of her. They'd circled the training area together so many times during their first week of classes that Lady was very familiar with the simple routine.

"What are the rest of you waiting for?" Hunt

Ryker, who'd been rummaging in the back of his truck, hopped down from the tailgate. "Take a lap, all of you."

The rumble of his baritone made Dallas's heart race as she ran past him. Keeping her eye on Lady, who was well ahead of her by now, she was grateful that the training center had invested in high-grade combat boots that were designed for running as well as walking. Otherwise, the backs of her ankles would've been sporting a pair of blisters by the time she neared the end of the wide ring.

Instead, she was merely working up the start of a sweat. To her relief, Haliburton had grudgingly joined in the run. Despite his delayed start, he was also the first of their classmates to finish. She could barely stand the guy, but she couldn't deny the fact that he packed some serious speed.

"Nice job!" she called softly as she ran past him and his dog across the finish line. Though she was sure he heard her, he refused to look up and acknowledge her. *Jerk!* She'd just finished saving his pride. *You're welcome.*

"Suit up!" Instructor Dawson barked, without giving them a chance to rest. "We'll be working with the bite sleeves first, and full suits later on." He rattled off their names to pair them up.

To her dismay, Haliburton was assigned as her partner. *Seriously?* Had neither instructor picked up on the fact that the guy had it in for her? Then again, maybe this was Hunt's idea of treating her with impartiality. *Just hope I live to talk about it.*

"You've got this!" Tracy murmured sympathetically as she marched past with her dog on a leash. She'd been paired up with one of the Evans twins. Sanchez had been paired with the other Evans twin.

Haliburton's upper lip curled as he stared after Tracy. "Already forming allies within the squad, are we?" He reached for his bite sleeve.

"I don't know what you're talking about." Dallas dragged on the heavily padded sleeve and secured it to her shoulder. "Last time I checked, all six of us were on the same team."

"Really?" he shot back tersely, "because from my perspective, only one out of six of us has been playing smoochy face with an instructor."

Though his words infuriated her, Dallas fell back on years of acting training to tone down her response. "Aw, do you want a kiss, Haliburton? Maybe I can put in a good word for you with one of my other doubles."

"What I want is a fair shot at graduating from this place," he snarled.

I'm not sure how standing on my eyeballs makes you any taller, but sure. "That makes two of us," she returned mildly. "So here's an idea. How about we work together to make it happen?"

His scowl deepened. "Why are you trying so hard to be my friend?"

It was an interesting question, coming from a man with so many layers of hostility rolling off of him. "Because I'm a friendly kinda gal," she mocked. "You might as well give in now. Most people are no match for my killer brand of friendliness."

"True." He smirked. "There are literally dozens of pictures online to prove it!"

Whatever. Knowing it was yet another snarky reference to the kiss she'd shared with Hunt Ryker, she waved a hand. "I'm not going to apologize for being a successful actress any more than I'm going to apologize for kicking your butt during the next exercise."

"In your dreams, Hollywood." He lifted his chin. "Just for the record, when you get bored playing cop and move on to your next gig, I'll still be saving lives."

Of all the spiteful, conceited, self-absorbed—! But before Dallas could come up with a worthy come-back, Instructor Dawson and Instructor Ryker waved them apart. The members of all three teams were directed to stand on opposite sides of the ring from their partners.

Dallas stood, fuming over the malicious way Haliburton was still smirking at her. Of all the rotten luck she'd ever had to endure, getting stuck working with him was the worst!

The two instructors marched between their ranks like soldiers. Their dogs pranced at their sides, awaiting their next orders. "No doubt you noticed that Instructor Ryker and I are not wearing our normal uniforms, nor were we present at the crack of five, though we broke a few speeding laws to get here. Would anyone like to take a look at our gear and venture a guess as to what we may have been up to?"

"You were in a parade!" Haliburton shouted.

Seriously? Dallas's stomach sank at the knowledge that he was going to continue riding her case about the kiss.

"This early in the morning?" Officer Dawson gave him a hard, searching look. "Not likely, trainee. Anyone have any better ideas?"

Tracy Miller's hand shot up.

He nodded at her to speak.

"Since there was a missing persons report on the local news stations last night, I'm going to guess you got called to help out with that."

"And you'd be right, Trainee Miller." He looked pointedly over his shoulder at Haliburton. "You might want to compare notes with your classmate over breakfast, Trainee Haliburton. Trainee Miller's contribution to the topic was significantly more relevant than yours." There was a warning note in his voice.

Haliburton retreated into sullen silence while Instructor Ryker took over. "Each of the vests we're wearing contains a first aid kit, CPR preparation kit, AED, emergency radio, flashlight, chemlight sticks, a pair of mylar blankets, and more." He spun in a circle to briefly hold each of their gazes. "Quick review. What's so important about the first forty-eight hours after a person goes missing?"

Trainee Sanchez's hand flew into the air. "After forty-eight hours, key witnesses start to forget stuff, and the overall chances of the missing person being found sorta tank."

"Bingo!" Instructor Ryker pointed with his thumb and forefinger. "So, to state it another way, it is crucial to locate missing people how soon after they go missing?"

"In the first forty-eight hours, sir."

"That's the purpose of this morning's training. We are going to unpack yet another resource to increase your chances of success in locating the next missing person you're tasked to find. As first responders, that includes training your dog in the all-important skills of scenting and tracking, which you covered in extensive detail with Instructor Dawson last week. The skill we are going to add to your arsenal this week is..." he slowly spun around again, making eye contact with each of them, "training your dog to attack in order to prevent or disrupt an assault."

He pulled on the bite sleeve he'd been holding at his side. "PoPo and I will demonstrate." First, he gave the command for his dog to sit and stay. Then he held up a hand and slowly retreated to roughly thirty feet away. Lowering his hand, he extended his arm encased in the bite sleeve and yelled, "Attack!"

PoPo flew across the training ring and leaped into the air to sink his teeth into the padded sleeve.

To Dallas's amazement, Instructor Ryker proceeded to yank his arm in every direction, as if trying to get away, and hollered as if he was being mortally injured.

At the end of the demonstration, he ordered his dog to sit and stay again while he explained. "In the event you find yourself in a situation that calls for an attack dog, trust me, the person your dog is attacking is not going to stand there in silence. So neither should you during this morning's exercise. Make the training realistic for your dog by kicking up a ruckus and genuinely trying to dislodge their hold on the bite sleeve."

Dallas and her classmates nodded in amazement and murmured in undertones to each other. A mix of anticipation and nervousness swirled across her tongue.

"Alright." Hunt clapped his hands three times to regain their attention. "I want to hear you yelling loud enough to wake the rest of your classmates back in the dorms."

Instructor Dawson jumped back into the conversation, bellowing, "All team members on the right, step at least ten yards away from your dogs. Then hold out your bite sleeves."

Dallas was one of the trainees standing on the right, so she held up her hand to keep Lady sitting. Then she slowly backed away from the dog and braced for the coming attack.

"Team members on the left, you will observe the first round of attacks and critique your teammates. You'll get your turn next, but wait for my command before you start. Since this is a training exercise, we're going to squeeze the maximum amount of learning from each segment of it. Are there any questions before we begin?" He treated each of them to another hard, piercing look. Then he raised one fist into the air. "Good. Ready, set, and go-o-o!" He pushed his arm through the air like a hammer as he lowered it to his side.

"Lady, attack!" Dallas let out a bloodcurdling scream when the Doberman Pinscher sank its teeth into her arm padding. Yanking back and forth with all of her strength, she tried to shake off her dog. It was both an exhilarating and exhausting exercise.

"Let go!" It finally dawned on Dallas that she would have to regain control of her dog, as both her owner and handler, to end the exercise. "Let go, Lady. Sit!" She had to repeat the command a few times to gain her dog's compliance. "Good girl," she panted. Reaching inside her pocket for a doggy bone snack, she rewarded Lady for a job well done. There was no doubt in her mind, or the mind of anyone else who'd been watching, that her dog had won their sparring exercise. She braced herself for another barrage of snide commentary from Haliburton.

He sidled across the ring in her direction. "Not bad, Hollywood," he drawled, giving her a lazy grin.

"Is that it?" she snapped, still gulping for air. "Maybe I'm a fool for expecting anything close to professionalism from you, but I was kinda hoping you'd manage to scrape up an actual critique." Heaven knew he loved to criticize others!

His smirk slipped. "Patience, Hollywood. I'm just getting started." His gaze took on a crafty glint. "Your acting wasn't too shabby, and I can see Lady putting a stop to an assault. Eventually."

My acting, huh? Not my dog handling. Not my cop skills. Not my hard work. "Sorry I asked."

He circled them critically. "Yep, your dog definitely has what it takes to learn."

My dog, not me. Dallas's panting slowed. "But you don't think I do, huh?"

"I never said that." He gave her another mocking grin. "However, if you want to see how the pros do it, watch and weep."

Gritting her teeth, she stared a hole between his shoulder blades as he swaggered away. *I hope your dog knocks you into Kingdom Come. I hope he swallows you whole for breakfast. I hope he sits back on his haunches and picks tiny Halliburton shreds from his teeth afterward.*

She received no such satisfaction, because

Haliburton and his dog proceeded to perform the exercise flawlessly. Again and again and again, until clusters of trainees crowded around the training ring on their way to the cafeteria to cheer him on. From the extra strut in his step as he humored them, it was clear that he thrived on having an audience.

Even more maddening, he managed to perform the exercise without having bits and pieces of grass get stuck in his hair, unlike Dallas, who was a complete wreck after a few clashes with Lady. By the time she and Tracy trudged their way to the cafeteria for breakfast, she was sporting multiple layers of dirt and grime. Plus, every muscle in her body was sore. No amount of gym workouts in the world could've prepared her for being mauled by her own dog.

"Do you think the instructors are trying to kill us?" A piteous groan eased out of her.

Tracy stretched her shoulders tiredly. "I dunno. Maybe. They did pair you with Haliburton." She shot Dallas a curiously searching look.

"I know," Dallas grumbled, "and as much as I can't stand the guy, I have to admit he's really good at the whole attack dog routine."

"Yeah, this is definitely not his first rodeo." Tracy sounded more admiring than irritated by that fact.

Dallas blinked at the tone of her classmate's voice. Unless she was mistaken, the woman was secretly crushing on the creep.

So much for Haliburton's fear that his classmates' sentiments were against him. It looked as if Tracy was more than a little impressed with his royal cockiness.

AFTER BREAKFAST, the training only got harder, especially after Instructor Dawson departed for a staff meeting. In his absence, Instructor Ryker ran the class one hair shy of merciless.

Once his students were garbed in full bite suits, he proceeded to let their dogs pummel the stuffing out of them. Only after each student performed the exercise to his nearly impossible expectations did he dismiss them one-by-one.

Haliburton was the first to leave, with his maddening smile stretching from one side of his smug face to the other. For once, he was too tired to linger and dole out his usual sarcastic commentary. Sanchez was dismissed next, then Miller, and eventually both of the Evans brothers.

"Come on, Trainee Hill. What's the hold up over there?" Instructor Ryker kept his voice brutally impersonal. "If you're too tired to finish the exercise, I can send you back to the dorm for a nap and we can pick up where we left off, say, around eight or nine o'clock tonight."

You wouldn't! Her lips parted in shock at his lack of empathy. "I'm not too tired, Instructor Ryker."

And do we really need to maintain such ridiculous formalities now that we're alone? She searched his features for any sign of human compassion — any hint at all of the man who'd once kissed her. She found nothing other than the same bland professionalism he'd given her classmates.

"Then what's the problem, trainee?"

Okay. Apparently, he had every intention of keeping up the formalities between them. *Too bad!* She swallowed a sigh of exhaustion. "Fine. I'll admit I'm a little tired, but that's not the problem. I think the hold up with Lady mastering this skill has something to do with the fact that I raised her from a pup. She's too loyal to cross certain lines with me, even during training." After the bite sleeve exercise, she'd all but lost interest in the simulation. Dallas could get her to run and leap at the bite suit, but not genuinely attack her while she was wearing it.

"If your theory is correct, then Lady needs to test out what she's learned on a new target."

Dallas nodded emphatically. "Yes, please. Maybe I could get one of my classmates to return to the ring for a few minutes."

"I have a better idea, trainee. One that might actually get us both to dinner before the cafeteria closes." He reached for the bite suit that Haliburton had discarded. "Send Lady after me."

"But Instructor Ryker—"

"Just do it, Dallas."

THE SECRET BABY RESCUE   79

Oh, my lands! For a second, she wasn't sure if she'd imagined him using her first name or what.

"Get your dog in position." He held her gaze as he backed up about twenty feet and bent into an expectant crouch. "Now imagine I'm about to commit the worst crime imaginable and give her the command to attack."

Mercy! The way he was looking at her was making her heart beat erratically. In the effort to gather her scattered senses, she had to close her eyes. *Focus, Dallas! What's the worst crime imaginable?*

Kidnapping, of course. And within that category of crimes, snatching innocent children ranked as the most dastardly. In fact, tracking down the fictional kidnappers in *A Girl With A Badge* was what had stirred her interest in pursuing a career in search and rescue operations.

For the sake of the exercise, she decided to imagine that Hunt Ryker was about to abduct a small child. Before she could over-think it, she snapped open her eyelids and shouted, "Lady, attack!"

She dashed after her dog, holding her hands out in front of her like she was clutching a weapon. "Get him, Lady," she urged. "Save the kid."

To her delight, Lady responded to the urgency in her voice and dashed for Hunt at maximum speed. She took a flying leap and hurtled her lithe body toward him. Snarling and growling, she dug into his padded sleeve with her teeth and pummeled his long frame with her hind legs.

"That's right, girl. You got 'em!"

Afterward, Dallas wasn't entirely certain if Lady actually succeeded in pulling Hunt to the ground, or if he simply gave the dog the win and voluntarily rolled with her. Either way, he ended up in the grass, with the dog snarling over him.

Dallas hastily gave the command for Lady to stand down.

"You did it," she crowed triumphantly, leaning forward to throw her arms around the Doberman. Maybe it was because she was so tired, or maybe it was because she was distracted by Hunt's look of pride, but Dallas sorely miscalculated her dog's movements. Their heads collided with a resounding crack.

For a moment, she saw stars. Then, with a gasp of pain, she rolled to the dirt.

"Dallas!" Hunt's face wavered over hers for a moment, coming in and out of focus. "Are you okay? Can you hear me?" There was a frantic edge to his voice. "How many fingers am I holding up?"

"Forty-five," she muttered dully. *I want to die. Please let me die.* There was nothing quite like making a complete and utter fool of oneself in front of the very guy one was trying to impress.

He chuckled in relief. "Yeah, you're still in there.

Seriously, though, how many fingers am I holding up, babe?"

"Babe?" The question came out as a squeak as his face came into better focus. "Oh, my lands! You totally lied about our kiss to Officer Dawson," she accused as she sat up. He'd known it was her when he'd kissed her — the real Dallas Hill and not one of her doubles.

"Would you rather I'd told him the truth?" Hunt gave her a hand to pull her to her feet.

"No." *Oh, golly!* Her head was aching so badly that she could barely stand up straight.

"Or the fact that I want to kiss you again right now?"

"Really?" She was so woozy that she sank back to one knee. "Is that why you never called me after the parade?"

"No." He blew out a resigned breath. "It was because I was busy getting my head screwed back on straight after the war. I thought you deserved better than a guy who had no idea what came next." He held out his hand again. "I didn't have a job at the time. Hadn't figured out where I was even going to live."

She stared at his long, capable fingers for a moment. "You never even gave us a chance," she whispered. *Or me.* She hadn't been looking for perfection. She had just been seeking a little confirmation that their kiss hadn't been entirely one-sided.

"I thought I was doing you a favor."

His confession sent so much joy rushing through her that it brought on an entirely different kind of dizziness. "I'm a lot tougher than I look, Hunt Ryker," she declared softly. Wow, but it felt wonderful to say that!

"Yeah, I'm starting to get that impression. I really hope you believe in giving a guy a second chance."

She squinted up at him through the pain lancing her temples. "Ask me again in twenty days, and you'll find out." In twenty days, she would graduate from the training center and be a free woman again. After Officer Dawson's warning, she was sure that no romantic entanglements would be tolerated between students and their instructors.

He was grimacing as he tugged her to her feet a second time. "Then it's going to be a long twenty days for me."

She smiled dreamily up at him, so he wouldn't have any reason to doubt what her answer was going to be.

"A very, very long twenty days," he sighed as his gaze dropped longingly to her mouth.

CHAPTER 5: A LITTLE DIGGING

HUNT

Over the next two weeks, Hunt settled into a rigorous routine of hard work and no play. When he wasn't training the recruits, he was training his dog. PoPo was still young and relatively inexperienced. He had a lot to learn, and the Texas Hotline Training Center provided endless opportunities for that. In addition to their state-of-the-art dog training ring, there were the track and scent trails to explore. Afterward, the burn ruins and city rubble provided a set of challenging routes in which to practice those skills.

Since Hunt was new to the facility and new to instructing, in general, he made a point of performing dry runs the evening before each training session to ensure that he and PoPo were prepared.

The few snatches of free time he could scrounge up, in and around all of his other responsibilities, he chose to spend at the training center's world-class gym. He felt a little guilty over the fact that he'd been too busy lately to keep up with the recommended physical therapy for his leg. According to the PT staff at Ft. Worth, he would only be able to maintain his leg's full range of movement if he continued their recommended workouts — literally forever.

Ultimately, it wasn't his guilt, however, that motivated him to resume his workouts. It was his discovery that Dallas reported to the gym at eight o'clock every evening.

Yeah, it was an odd way to start dating a woman, but it was the only option he had available at the moment. He tugged on a pair of black lycra running pants to hide the crisscross of scars on his legs. Then he shrugged on a white compression shirt to emphasize his ripped upper body. *My one good feature.*

Since he lived on site, it would've taken about the same time to drive and find a parking spot as it did to cut across the campus on foot, so he often to begin his workout with a quick jog to the gym.

Once inside, he positioned himself at one of the Nautical weight machines near the entrance, so he wouldn't miss Dallas's arrival. Stacking the weight to a number guaranteed to make his biceps bulge, he made sure he was pumping lead the moment she walked in.

He was pretty sure her flush deepened a little when she nodded a greeting at him. It was hard to tell, since she was already pink from exertion. She always started her evening gym workouts with a run around the biggest lake. She was already sweaty, too, something the Marine in him found particularly attractive. A girl who wasn't afraid to sweat. *Yeah, baby!*

Unlike several of her other classmates who came to the gym on the prowl in skimpy outfits, however, she was all business in a pink sleeveless top, black yoga pants, and bluetooth earbuds. He discreetly watched her as she made her way around the gym. Tonight was Saturday. If he remembered correctly from last week, she would be doing upper body training.

She started off with a round of arm curls, which she performed in such perfect rhythm that he was pretty sure she was working out to music. It made him burn with curiosity to find out what artists she listened to. Pop? Rock? Country? Christian? He couldn't wait to find out.

For most of her workout, she ignored him. Or pretended to. He could feel her eyes on him a few times when she thought he wasn't looking, but once he got lucky and managed to ensnare her beautiful blue gaze for a few seconds.

He caressed her with his gaze and was rewarded with another blush. Glancing covertly around the gym, he hoped he was being subtle for the sake of anyone who might be watching them. However, he didn't care one bit that Dallas probably understood that he was shamelessly flirting with her.

He finished earlier than he expected and lingered at the end of his workout, drawing it out until Dallas was finished with hers. Since he couldn't walk her back to her dorm or kiss her goodnight, finishing at the same time was the best he could do to end their "date."

After she shyly waved goodbye, he tossed his sweat towel over his shoulder and moseyed his way back to his townhouse to finish his day the same way he always did — by spending a few hours on his laptop investigating the whereabouts of his two missing Marine buddies.

The rest of the world might be content to let Marcus Zane and Digby MacLamore fade into the sunset of their memories, but not him. *Never!* He wasn't going to stop looking until someone produced their remains. And so far, that hadn't happened.

He and Marcus had first met during their deployment to Afghanistan. He and Dig went further back — much further back. All the way to basic training, to be exact. Like him, Dig had gone on to serve as an MP. Dig had also gone on to become his brother-in-law. Jillian's missing husband. JT's missing father. Hunt had every reason in the world to find the man, and then some.

After he showered and changed, he pulled back the navy comforter of his king-sized bed and attempted to nudge PoPo to one side of the white sheets, a gesture that nearly always failed. As expected, PoPo simply waited until Hunt was propped against his pillows. Then the dog rolled across his legs to continue snoozing.

"You're such a brat!" Hunt knew he should insist on more discipline. A proper service dog should sleep in a cage.

PoPo cracked one eyelid open and yawned loudly.

Someday I'm gonna be sharing this bed with my wife, you blasted mutt. Hunt shook his head, wondering where that thought had come from. A lovely, sculpted face took shape in his mind, one that had been making his heart pound ever since the kiss she'd planted on him.

Shoot! They weren't even officially dating yet. It was way too soon to be dreaming about stuff like that. What a crazy incredible thing it would be, though, to have a woman like Dallas Hill sitting across from him at the breakfast table each morning, training dogs with him during the day, and cuddled in his arms at night.

Hunt rubbed a hand across his face. *First things first.* She needed to graduate from the Texas Hotline Training Center first. Then he needed to ask her out, and she needed to say yes. Then, and only then, could they move forward to the bigger and better stuff — things that started with forever and ended with always.

In an attempt to distract himself from the overwhelming desire to pick up his phone and dial her right now, Hunt scowled his way through his meager notes on Marcus and Digby. He truly hated what little information he'd uncovered so far concerning their current status. Both were still classified as missing in action, which made little sense. This was the grand old USA, for Pete's sake! Surely, fifteen months was long enough for the greatest nation in the world to recover the remains of a few fallen soldiers. So why hadn't they?

Which made him circle back to the same insane hope he entertained every evening before falling asleep. What if Marcus and Dig were still alive?

Quite frankly, he was growing tired of hearing the same sorry excuses over email from the few folks in uniform willing to correspond with him. *Not likely to recover their remains due to the explosion. Not likely to recover their remains due to Marcus's fall from the cliff. Not likely to recover their remains due to the dangers of leading a search for them through enemy territory. Not likely. Not likely. Not likely.*

Well, "not likely" wasn't good enough for the loved ones these two men had left behind! Nobody just disappeared for good. Even people who fell from cliffs could most certainly be recovered...eventually.

They could be swept downstream and beached miles away. They could be scraped from valleys below or ledges on the way down.

Ledges. That gave Hunt an idea. Since he'd been in the thick of the battle where both men had gone missing, he knew exactly where their unit had been located on the map — the exact mountain pass that had been used to trap him and his fellow Marines like rats during the ambush. In fact, he knew the exact cliff that Axel Hammerstone claimed he and Marcus had been hanging from before Marcus had let go and plummeted to his death.

In a burst of energy, Hunt pulled up a satellite image and zoomed in on the mountain pass and cliff wall in question. Then he slowly scrolled his way down the cliff in a zig-zagging motion. Maybe he was just grasping at straws, but he'd yet to run across any natural-formed cliff that didn't possess a few aberrations and outcroppings. It took a few minutes for him to find what he was looking for.

There! The ledge practically reached out from his computer screen and slapped him in the face when it finally popped into view. *Boom shakalaka!* Using the map legend, Hunt estimated the ledge was protruding anywhere from twenty to forty feet below the cliff's edge. However, considering that both missing men were about six feet tall, that would've put Marcus roughly twelve feet closer to the ledge when he'd let go of Axel Hammerstone's ankles —

assuming, of course, that the men had been dangling over the ledge, as opposed to some place else along the cliff.

Yeah, that was a whole lot of what if's, but listening to the realists hadn't resulted in any definitive answers. Hunt was more than ready to start grasping at straws. And miracles. Especially miracles.

If Marcus Zane had, in fact, fallen to a ledge instead of the bottom of the cliff, it opened up a whole new set of possibilities. One was that he'd fallen as far as twenty-eight feet to the ledge Hunt had his eyes glued to right now. A second possibility was that Marcus had fallen as little as eight feet to the same blasted ledge.

And Hunt had never heard of anyone dying from an eight-foot drop. He gave a whoop of delight that had PoPo whipping his head up in alarm to blink sleepily at him.

"I think we're onto something here, Po!" He playfully swatted the dog on his rump.

Seeing nothing worthy of his canine attention, PoPo merely yawned again and rolled to his other side, still sprawled across Hunt's calves.

Trying not to disturb the sleeping dog, Hunt stretched for his cell phone, which was recharging on his nightstand, and managed to retrieve it without unseating the dog.

Mashing Axel's speed dial button, he waited impatiently while the phone rang.

His friend picked up on the third ring. "Dude! It's past eleven o'clock. Pretty sure there are laws against bothering people this late," he teased.

"Nah, that only applies to cold callers, and I have something hot off the grill to share."

"Oh, it's definitely too late for puns." Axel groaned.

"Aw! Are you in bed already, princess?"

"Yes," a female voice snapped. "If that's Hunt Ryker again, so help me, you better tell him..."

The rest of what Axel's wife said sounded like it was muffled by a kiss.

"I'm still here." He pretended to gag.

There was a brief scuffle, a few chuckles, and another kiss. This time it was a loud, exaggerated smooch into the phone that he had no doubt was intended for his benefit.

Then Axel was back. "My wife says to tell you if you don't want to hear more of that, then you shouldn't be dialing newlyweds this late."

"It's not that late," Hunt protested, "and it's important. Please assure your lovely bride I wouldn't have called if it wasn't."

"Or," Axel countered with a snicker, "you can explain it to her in person on Monday, now that you work at the same place."

Thanks, but I'd rather not. Kristi Hammerstone

worked as a K9 search and rescue instructor for the center's bedrock dog handler certification program. Hunt's few encounters with her had proven that she was as tough as she was beautiful. A real pistol.

Ignoring his friend's suggestion, Hunt tried a different tactic. "Listen, Axe. I, uh, just texted you a few pictures. Need you to take a look at them."

"Yeah," his friend sighed. "I'm already looking at them." He didn't sound too thrilled about that fact.

"It's a ledge."

"I can see that, Hunt."

"On a cliff in Kandahar, bro."

"I don't like where this is going. Hang on a sec." There were muffled voices in the background, then the opening and shutting of a door. "Okay, I just stepped outside. It's just you and me, man, so if you need to talk—"

"That's what I've been trying to tell you," Hunt growled. "According to my satellite map, there's a really good chance that this particular ledge was only about twenty to forty feet below where your fingers were hanging from—"

"Stop!" Axel's voice was harsh with emotion. "Just stop, alright?"

"Why?" Hunt was aghast at his friend's tone. "Don't you see what this means? Marcus could be alive."

"But he's not."

"You don't know that," Hunt exploded. "I just presented you with a very plausible possibility."

"I don't live by possibilities, man, and neither should you. They'll tear you apart. I should know. I ran through every blasted one of them while I was lying in that blasted hospital bed. Nearly lost my mind in the process." Axel's voice cracked.

"Hey! Whoa! I wasn't trying to make you re-live the nightmare. Far from it. I was trying to give you hope." *I was trying to give all of us hope.* Hunt gripped the screen of his laptop with both hands. *And that hope is staring us both in the face right now.* Why couldn't Axel see that?

"It's false hope. Trust me, Hunt. There's nobody in the universe who wants Marcus back more than I do." Axel stopped and cleared his throat. "Listen, I've finally made my peace with everything that happened that day, and you need to do the same."

Hunt felt close to weeping at the finality in his friend's voice. "So that's it? What about our motto? No man left behind?"

"Don't do this, please?" Axel cleared his throat again. "Where's all this coming from, anyway? I thought I talked you into getting a new job so you could make a fresh start like I did. Are things not working out for you here at the training center?"

"No, they're good." *I get it. You think I'm still messed up in the head, but you're wrong.* Maybe if he could convince Axel he was okay, he'd be willing to listen. "More than good, actually. I like it here. Enough that I can see myself staying for a while."

"Glad to hear it. That's what you need to focus on. All the good stuff. All the things that are going right." Axel's voice turned sly. "That, and it's about time to nudge you back into the dating game."

"Ouch! You don't think I'm capable of cruising chicks on my own?" Hunt hadn't intended to borrow one of Marcus's favorite phrases, but it slipped out. *In for a penny.* "I learned from the best, you know. We both did." By the best, he meant Marcus, of course. Just thinking about the guy never failed to make him smile. Marcus had it going on when it came to the ladies. A special brand of charm that he'd never been shy about pouring on.

"Yep. He's unforgettable, Hunt. Believe me, I'm not trying to forget him. I'm just trying to keep living. It's what he would have wanted."

True, but Marcus still wouldn't have given up on his friends if their roles were reversed. However, Hunt didn't feel like it was the right time to point that out. Apparently, Axel's anguish over losing Marcus was still too raw and too deep.

Guess I should have thought this through a little better before picking up the phone. It only made sense that Axel was taking the loss of Marcus harder than most people. The two of them had been best friends since high school, and Axel was still pretty tight with

Marcus's parents and sister. Not to mention, he was the last person to see Marcus alive.

Hunt could only imagine the nightmares Axel had dealt with as he lived and re-lived the way he and Marcus had been blasted over the edge of that cliff during the ambush in Kandahar. It was Axel's grip on the edge that had kept the two of them from immediately plunging to their deaths, and it had been Marcus's grip on Axel's ankles that would have eventually pulled the two of them the rest of the way over. According to Axel, Marcus had instead yelled *Semper Fi*, and let go — sacrificing himself to buy a little extra time for the rescuers to reach his best friend.

"You're right." Hunt gave himself a mental shake. "Marcus would've wanted us to keep living." Which he fully intended to do *while* continuing to hunt down his whereabouts. Maybe Axel was too close to the situation to do what needed to be done, but Hunt wasn't. If that meant he was going to have to continue his manhunt alone, so be it.

There was a long pause on the other end of the line. "So tell me about this chick cruising you've apparently been doing on your own." Axel sounded amused. "To be honest, I was kind of expecting you to hook up with Dallas Hill for a while there. That was *some* kiss the paparazzi caught on camera during your welcome home parade."

"A movie star, huh?" Hunt kept his voice light

and teasing. "That's the kind of gal you'd pair me up with?"

"Hey, I saw what I saw in the picture." Axel chuckled knowingly. "So did tens of thousands of other people."

"Well, according to the press, the woman I kissed wasn't the real Dallas. It was one of her doubles."

"Guess I missed that part."

Hunt grinned as he tipped his head back against his pillows. "But I'm happy to say that they were dead wrong. She's the real deal, man."

There was a moment of dramatic silence before Axel started sputtering. "Real deal! As in the present tense?"

"Maybe."

"You mean there's actually something going on between you and Dallas Hill?" Axel sounded so incredulous that Hunt wondered if he should be in insulted.

"It's complicated."

"Shoot, man! You called *me*. So spill!"

"I think I'm in love," Hunt confessed.

"That's huge! Not sure what's so complicated about it, though. Have you told her?"

"No can do. She's a student in my class right now."

"No way!" Axel gave a long, low whistle.

"Way. I'm not sure how closely you've been following her career, but here's the short version. She left show biz to attend the police academy, and now she's here at the Texas Hotline Training Center getting credentialed in search and rescue operations."

"Okay, I'm starting to see the complicated part about your love life, bro."

"Warned you."

"An actress who ended up on the police force." Axel sounded puzzled. "You don't see that happen very often."

Never. You see it never. Hunt was well aware of how special Dallas was. "Yep, she's determined to save the world, one missing person at a time."

"Are you drooling on your phone?" Axel gave a delighted chuckle. "Because you sure sound like it."

"Maybe. Drooling is about all I'm allowed to do right now." Hunt gave a loud, frustrated groan that made PoPo jump. Issuing a bark of protest, the dog rolled off his legs and buried his head under the covers.

"Yeah, that's rough. Been there, done that, and gone through the excruciating pain of collecting that t-shirt," Axel informed him a little too cheerfully. "Except I was the student, and Kristi got to play boss lady as my instructor." He snickered. "Most frustrating few weeks of my entire life, but it was also really hot! Not gonna lie about that."

"Not helping," Hunt grumbled.

"Wasn't trying to," his friend shot back. "I'm too

busy enjoying your discomfort and celebrating the fact that I'm no longer in your shoes."

"Gosh! With friends like you..."

"Hey, you're the one who called."

"Yeah, well, we all have regrets," Hunt scoffed.

"Uh-huh. Something tells me you'll still expect me to pick up the phone the next time you dial in the middle of the night and interrupt my married bliss."

"I'm hanging up now."

"If Kristi were out here on the back porch with me, she would thank you for that."

With a snort of laughter, Hunt disconnected the line. *Well, that conversation didn't go as planned.* He had to give Axel some credit, though. The guy had always been there for him, putting up with his garbage and offering moral support throughout his lengthy hospital stay. He'd listened to Hunt's anger at the world, his million and one gripes about how much pain he was in, along with his mountain of uncertainties about leaving the military and finding his way in the civilian world again. Plus, Axel had been the one to inform him about the job listing at the Texas Hotline Training Center. He really owed the guy.

Reaching down to scratch PoPo behind the ears, he scrolled again through the screenshots he'd taken of the cliff in Kandahar. PoPo made a muttering sound in the back of his throat and rolled over beneath the blankets.

A tiny sliver of blue in one of the photos made Hunt pause and stare. *What in the world?* He lifted his laptop screen and tilted it from side to side, trying to get a better look at the strange object. One thing was for sure. Nothing the color of blue was native to that sandy, rocky terrain. Whatever it was, it had to be man-made.

Zooming in didn't help much. It only made the photo more pixely. Blowing out a frustrated breath, Hunt painstakingly went back to work on the satellite map, zooming in from different angles to take more screenshots.

His heart thumped harder as he examined each one and came to the conclusion that he was looking at a blue chemlight — the kind a person breaks during an emergency and uses to flag down help. It could only mean one thing. Someone, at some point in time, had been stranded on that ledge, calling for help.

Though the discovery in no way proved that Marcus was alive, it did prove something noteworthy. The ledge was wide enough to hold a human body, which meant that Hunt was no longer simply grasping at straws. He was staring at the very real possibility that Marcus had survived his fall.

Since Axel wasn't in the frame of mind to deal with the frantic brand of hope coursing through Hunt's veins, it might be best to keep this latest lead to himself — at least until he could follow it and see where it led.

Close to choking from excitement, he shot the series of photographs in an email to a few key military personnel, who might be in the position to dig a little deeper into the matter. It had been so long since the last time he'd reached out to them that he wasn't certain if their email addresses were still current. Regardless, Hunt took the time to copy his former company commander, battalion commander, brigade commander, and their non-commissioned officers. He even took the time to look up the contact information for the United States Marine Corps Criminal Investigative Division and copied them, too.

At worst, they would write him off as an ex-soldier experiencing some sort of mental breakdown. At best, they might take a look at the photos and do a little investigating of their own. Regardless, Hunt felt like he owed it to Marcus to at least try to be heard.

I'm not going to leave you behind, buddy. One way or the other, I'm going to find you and bring you home. Hunt could only hope and pray he wasn't simply digging up more heartache for everyone he knew and loved.

CHAPTER 6: SIMULATION EXERCISE

DALLAS

Last day of training

"Today will be our final training exercise," Instructor Hunt Ryker barked in his best drill sergeant voice that Dallas found completely swoon-worthy. She watched him from beneath her lashes as he stalked with military decisiveness in front of her and her classmates, while describing the requirements of their final challenge. They were standing in the staging area outside the main auditorium. A large black SUV with tinted windows was idling nearby with its doors standing open. It contained all six of their dogs in their cages, plus the equipment they would be allowed to use during the scenario.

My very last training exercise. Dallas and her classmates traded excited glances. It was a huge milestone to have reached this point — to have survived the rigors of the prestigious Texas Hotline Training Center. Well, almost. They had one final challenge to complete.

As hard as she tried to focus on what Hunt was saying, Dallas couldn't keep her thoughts from drifting to how lucky she was that she and Hunt had gotten to spend the last month of their lives at the training center together, getting to know each other in ways that some couples never got to know each other.

She'd gotten to witness firsthand how hard he worked, how both demanding and patient he could be with his students, and how impeccable his work ethic was. He'd kept his promise to Officer Dawson, too, by keeping things unquestionably and painfully professional between them in class. He'd done more than his fair share of silent flirting from a distance, though. The way he looked at her during their gym workouts had kept her on the edge of crazy for nearly five weeks straight. She was seriously dying to be in his arms again. Not once, though, had he called, texted, touched, or put any moves on her.

Instead, he'd continued to push her and her classmates to their maximum potential, day in and day out.

And today would be no exception. Her heartbeat sped in anticipation of another grueling exercise. If Jug Dawson was letting Hunt take the lead, she and her classmates were all but guaranteed to spend their day sweaty and dirty. They would be exhausted at the end, but exhilarated about what they'd learned. It was always that way when Hunt was in charge. He was an all-or-nothing kind of guy. It was one of the biggest things she loved about him.

Love? Dallas pressed a hand to her racing heart, wondering where that thought had come from. They weren't even dating yet, and they'd only kissed one time, but...

"You still alive over there, Trainee Hill?" Hunt's harsh voice cut through her daydreams, bringing her crashing back to reality.

She blinked and forced her attention back to him. "Yes, sir."

His answering glare made her flush with embarrassment.

A-a-a-nd I'm no longer in love with you. It was only a short-lived brainstorm. I'm fully recovered. She straightened her shoulders, hating the way he'd called her out like that in front of her classmates. She hated herself even more for giving him reason to.

"Good, because your teammates probably wouldn't appreciate me sending the whole pack of you on a lap around the field just to wake you up."

"You'd be right, sir." Haliburton shot Dallas one of his infuriating, knowing smirks, which told her he'd probably guessed exactly where her mind had been wandering.

She glared back at Hunt. *Now I want to slap you*

more than kiss you. Well done, Staff Sergeant. Keep it up, and there may not be another kiss. Ever.

Jaw clenched, he continued his speech. "As I was saying before Trainee Hill's mind started to wander, we'll be searching for a missing girl in the city rubble."

We're simulating a missing child case? Finally! Her senses snapped to full alertness while she choked down a mouthful of guilt. No wonder Hunt was so irritated by her lack of attention. Not only was she zoning out during an important briefing, which was both irresponsible and disrespectful on her part, she'd almost missed the fact that he'd custom-tailored his final lesson to her dream job. There was nothing she wanted to do more than spend the rest of her life searching for and finding missing children.

Okay. You win! Way to make me fall in love with you all over again! She could tell by the way he was looking at her that he wasn't really mad at her. He only wanted her one hundred percent tuned into his safety briefing for all the right reasons.

He waved a hand. "Here are the details of the case. Mary Harkins went missing from her fenced-in backyard yesterday evening around six-fifteen. She's three-years-old. Her mother was making dinner on the other side of the kitchen window and swears she only took her eye off her daughter for a few seconds while she put something in the oven."

Dallas's heart sank at how typical the scenario was. A few seconds was all it took for a trolling stranger to reach over the fence, grab a child, and take off.

"Mrs. Harkins said when she turned back around, she noticed the gate was open, and her daughter was missing. She rushed outside, calling her name, and discovered the child's favorite stuffed animal lying on the ground. It's a toy Mary is rarely seen without and would have never voluntarily left it behind. The sight of it made Mrs. Harkins dial 911."

Dallas glanced at her classmates again, struck by how serious their expressions were. She wondered if it was because they realized that the next briefing they received would involve a real emergency.

"So far," Hunt continued tersely, "the local police and two volunteer search and rescue teams have canvassed every neighborhood within a five-mile radius and are slowly working their way outward. Additionally, the tip line just received an interesting call about the sighting of a small girl who meets Mary's description. She was being carried by a man into a vacant warehouse on the edge of town. The building is condemned, scheduled for demolition, and is a known hotspot for drug deals." He paused for a few seconds to let his listeners absorb what they'd heard. "This is where you come in. Your team has been called in to follow up on this latest lead. You've been cautioned to assume that any individuals you encounter in this warehouse are armed and dangerous."

Haliburton's hand shot up. "Will our team go in alone, or will we be accompanied by local law enforcement officials?"

Hunt shook his head gravely. "In an ideal world? Yes, you'd have all kinds of backup, but this isn't an ideal world, is it? The local PD is over budget and stretched about as thin as a single unit can be stretched. One deputy is out handling a three-car pileup. The fire department and EMTs are currently processing the same call. Another deputy is filing a report on a break-in at a pawn shop downtown. You're lucky to have scraped up the six search and rescue professionals you're going in with."

"Got it." Haliburton frowned in concentration, his clever mind undoubtedly running over every possible scenario.

Tracy Miller's hand flew up next. "Are you assigning us fictional backgrounds, or will we be approaching this exercise from our real-life perspectives?"

"Great question, Trainee Miller. The answer is both. During this exercise, you'll be operating like a real-life TEXSAR team, using your actual expertise. In this scenario, you get to be the one EMT the ambulatory department was able to spare. Trainee Hill, you got called in from the city to help out. Trainee Evans and Trainee Evans, you'll be representing the fire department. Trainee Sanchez, you're the state trooper driving through town on a trip home from visiting your folks. You see the amber alert and decide to help out. Trainee Haliburton, you're the senior law enforcement official present, so you'll be heading up the team. Are there any other questions?"

Dallas and her classmates shook their heads.

"Okay. From this moment forward, I will simply observe and grade you, as well as step in to handle any real emergencies. No more questions will be permitted until the end of the exercise. For all intents and purposes, I am officially invisible." He held up a timer and clicked a button. "The clock is now ticking."

"Huddle up, kids!" Haliburton gave a lofty twirl of his finger, clearly enjoying the fact that he'd been put in charge.

Resisting the urge to roll her eyes, Dallas crowded closer, pretty sure she was going to get the worst assignment. Throughout the program, Haliburton had taken special delight in torturing her. No matter how hard she worked, he never seemed to take her seriously. To him, she was no more than a bored celebrity looking for a little excitement.

Oh, well. In one more day, he would no longer be her problem.

"We'll enter the warehouse in pairs, since there's a good chance we may encounter a few thugs."

Haliburton's smirk disappeared as he spread a map of the building on the ground in front of them. "Evans and Miller, you'll take the front entrance. Evans and Sanchez, you'll take the back entrance. Hill, you're with me. You and I will enter through the parking garage."

Lucky me! I get to spend my last few hours of training being harassed by you. Her eyebrows rose in challenge. "I thought the garage was collapsed." They'd puttered around the ruins a few times before, and she recalled the parking garage being a pile of concrete and twisted metal.

Though he gave her a rigid nod, his expression didn't change. "It is. With a little elbow grease, though, I think we can clear a path to the double doors. It'll throw off whoever's inside, since they won't be expecting anyone to come at them from that direction."

Elbow grease. Yippee! My day keeps getting better. She could think of nothing less exciting than lugging around jagged pieces of concrete. Not to mention it would be dirty, sweaty work. Apparently, Haliburton was geared up to deliver her an extra dose of punishment today.

She glanced at her watch. It was eight in the morning, and Hunt never extended their training beyond the dinner hour. So, at worst, she only had to endure Haliburton's cocky attitude for ten more hours. *Ten more hours...ugh!* It might as well have been ten more years. She pressed two fingers to her lips to suppress a whimper of self-pity.

Haliburton noted her gesture with a curled lip. "Are you as excited as I am about this, Hollywood?"

"You have no idea," she retorted blandly.

When he wasn't looking, Tracy squeezed her hand. "This is the last time you have to put up with him," she whispered. "You've got this!"

They bumped fists before jogging to the SUV to climb aboard.

Sanchez drove, while Instructor Ryker rode shotgun, quietly observing their every move.

Dallas took it upon herself to inspect her and Haliburton's safety gear as Sanchez rolled the vehicle from the parking lot. "Uh...*El Capitan*, I have some bad news. The battery in your radio is dead. Anybody have a spare?"

"What the—?" He snatched it from her hand and fiddled with the knobs. "You gotta be kidding me. You'd think they'd check to make sure we have proper gear for this stuff."

"I think dealing with malfunctioning equipment is part of the exercise." Tracy's observation earned her a scorching glare from their team leader.

He barked out a question. "What kind of batteries does it take?"

"Rechargeable ones, actually." Excited by the discovery, Dallas unzipped the pockets of her borrowed safety vest to search through each one.

"Oo, I just found a cord. Someone, try plugging this into the dashboard and see what happens."

One of the Evans twins leaned forward to fiddle with the controls on the dashboard. To their enormous luck, the SUV was equipped with a cigarette lighter adaptor plug. "We have a flashing red light," he reported gleefully. "I think that means it's getting juice."

"Uh-oh," Dallas muttered a few seconds later.

"Now, what?" Haliburton didn't look too thrilled.

"We have a flashlight on the blink." It was his, as well, though she was careful not to infer that it was his fault. It could have happened to any of them. She had no doubt Hunt Ryker was going to point that fact out at the end of the day. They were all equally guilty of not checking their equipment before they left the staging area, and the rules were that they couldn't return to the staging area until the end of the exercise. They were supposed to pretend like they were hours away from home base the moment they drove out of the parking lot.

Haliburton leaned closer to her and hissed. "Are you trying to flunk us?"

She ignored him. "It takes three C batteries. Everyone, scrub your area of the van for spare batteries." Sanchez hastily pulled over to the curb to help out, but a quick search brought them up empty.

"Let's keep moving," Haliburton snarled.

"Or you could drop me off at the gas station real quick." Dallas pointed out the window at the service station located right outside the training center's campus. "They usually have quick-grab items like batteries. It'll only take two snaps."

Shaking his head in irritation, Haliburton gave the motion to do as she requested. In less than two minutes, she hopped back inside the SUV, waving a package of batteries. "Success!"

"Buckle up!" Haliburton gave her a hard, searching look.

She considered ignoring it, but was unable to bring herself to do so. "Now, who's in a hurry to get started?" She mimicked his insult from earlier as she buckled her seatbelt. Then she quickly replaced his batteries and flashed the light directly in his eyes.

He flinched.

"See? It works," she informed him sweetly. "You're welcome, *El Capitan*."

"Stop calling me that!"

"Oh, are we using our real names today?" She pretended innocence. "Mine is Dallas Hill, in case you weren't aware. Not Hollywood, not Shiny Badge, and not Hey You."

"Burn," Sanchez chortled from the front seat. "She just nailed you to the wall, bro."

Everyone except Haliburton laughed. If looks could kill, his dark expression would have planted her six feet beneath the pavement they were driving on.

It suddenly dawned on her that he was truly embarrassed to be repeatedly called out in front of their classmates the way she was doing. Yeah, he could be a real jerk sometimes — make that *all* the time, but he took genuine pride in his work. Being a police officer really meant something to him. Plus, he was her partner for the day, and here she was acting like, well...*him*.

Swallowing weeks of pent up irritation with him, she breathlessly announced, "All joking aside, I've got your back today, Haliburton. Promise." She held out a fist, mentally pleading with him to accept her peace offering.

After a moment's hesitation, he popped her fist with his. "You better, Holly—er, Hill."

His near slip-up earned him another round of snickers. "Hill's just so short," he protested, turning red. "It needs more syllables or something."

"How about Officer Hill, then?" she suggested quietly.

He nodded grudgingly. "I reckon you've earned that one."

"You bet I have, sheriff!" It was the first time she'd ever used his official title, and the way he straightened his shoulders when she said it told her all she needed to know. He appreciated it. *Okay. New tactic.* Apparently, treating Haliburton with a little respect was all he really craved. It was too bad she hadn't tried that weeks ago. They'd wasted way too much valuable time throwing barbs at each other.

Sanchez braked at the edge of the field that housed the city rubble. "Alright, folks," he noted in satisfaction. "It's game time!"

"Radio silence," Haliburton ordered as they piled from the vehicle with their weapons and gear. He used hand motions to instruct them to collect their dogs. Then he passed around a rumpled polka dot sweatshirt that supposedly belonged to the child they were searching for. They took turns allowing their dogs to sniff it and pick up the child's scent.

Zipping the sweatshirt inside his backpack, Haliburton motioned for them to move in pairs toward the building. Even when Instructor Ryker branched off to follow Evans and Miller's team for a while, Haliburton continued to maintain his silence with her. It was Dallas's cue that he intended to follow the scenario to the T.

Works for me. She did her best to watch and accurately interpret his hand motions, though sometimes she wasn't entirely sure what he was trying to communicate. He seemed to have a language of his own, not always sticking to the by-the-book signals. Fortunately, it was Haliburton. There wasn't much about him that was overly complicated to interpret.

Biting her lower lip, Dallas suffered his quirky signals in silence as he directed them to lug away blocks of jagged concrete to clear a path through the collapsed parking garage. It took them nearly half an hour to create a hole big enough to squeeze their way through one of the doors. By the time they stepped into the dim interior of the condemned city building, they were sweating profusely.

Dallas waved a hand at her face. *I love my job. I love my job.*

A shot sounded nearby, making her tense.

Haliburton tugged her down to the floor beside him, then deliberately moved in front of her to run point.

Seriously? Now you're going to play macho man? Then again, his unexpected show of protectiveness was better than being used as a human shield. It took several more seconds for her eyesight to adjust to the darkness.

It appeared they were crouched inside some sort of office. Several ceiling tiles were caved in, dumping insulation and wires onto the mattress of the bed below.

Wait! What was a mattress doing in an office? She silently noted how all the appliances were pulled away from their wall sockets. The television was facing the wall, and the only lamp in the room was lying on its side. A thick layer of dust coated everything — from the bookshelves to the carpet.

Only one item was free of the dust. Dallas's eyes widened to note it was a child's pink, unlaced sneaker. She pointed, but Lady was already sniffing her way toward the shoe. Haliburton's K9 partner, a brown Rottweiler named Bruiser, joined her. Both dogs whined to indicate it was a match to the child's scent they were tracking. Then the canines continued snuffling their way toward the door.

Haliburton grinned and gave Dallas a thumbs up.

Though it was only a training exercise, she felt a lurch of excitement at the knowledge that they'd successfully located the trail of their target. No, not a target. She was a three-year-old girl named Mary, who'd been snatched from her own backyard. Dallas had every intention of finding and restoring the kid to her mother.

Haliburton signaled her to follow the dogs.

A few minutes later, they met up with the rest of their team in the center of the warehouse, "arrested" two thugs on drug possession charges, and relieved them of their weapons. However, they failed to locate the missing little girl.

"It doesn't make sense." Since they'd successfully cleared the building, Haliburton ended their radio silence. He paced back and forth across the dusty room. "The girl's scent is all over the place. We found her shoes, her hair ribbon, a discarded PB&J sandwich with a child-sized bite mark. What are we missing? Start talking."

Dallas, who was eyeing their two "detainees,"

noticed them give each other a speaking glance. Even though they were pretending to be users who were stoned out of their heads, her gut told her they knew something vital to the exercise.

"Sheriff, with your permission, I'd like to take a crack at our witnesses." She eyed the two men curiously.

"You can go as many rounds as you like with them back at the station, officer."

"I'd rather do it now," she insisted. "I have an angle I'd like to work."

"Does anyone else have any other ideas besides negotiating with a pair of crackheads?" Hands on his hips, he surveyed the group with exasperation.

When no one answered him, Dallas slipped away from the huddle. Crackheads or not, their two captives were witnesses. And right now, they were the only leads her team had. Though she slowed her steps as she approached them, they muttered and made jerky movements, clearly indicating her proximity was making them uncomfortable.

"Hi. My name is Dallas, like the city. What's your name?"

They muttered some more and looked everywhere but at her. Their clothing was tattered and dirty, and their faces were smudged with the same dust that coated the rest of the building.

"Listen, I could really use your help. I'm trying

to find a little girl. Her name is Mary, and she's lost. I want to take her home to her mother."

Neither man acted like they understood her.

In a burst of inspiration, Dallas started to cry. "I'm so sorry," she sobbed, pretending to wipe her nose. "I'm just so scared for little Mary."

Both men turned to stare at her. "Do you have any kids?" she quavered.

One of the men gave her a jerky head shake. *Negative.*

"A little sister, maybe?" She sniffled loudly.

One of them nodded hesitantly. "Me, too." She started sobbing again, even louder than before. "Mary is my sister, and I'm so scared I'm never going to see her again." Reaching inside her trousers to produce a grimy photo of the small child, she held it up for them to peer at. "Have you seen her?"

The two men looked at each other. The same one who'd nodded before, nodded again.

"Is she in the building?"

The men cast furtive glances across the room at the other uniformed officers, as if fearful of saying anything else in front of them.

She quickly stepped between them, blocking their line of sight, and held up the picture again. "Please," she begged tearfully. "You're the only one who can help me. I'm afraid the man who took my little sister is going to hurt her." She lowered her voice and put a hand over her mouth to confide in a choked voice. "If you help me, I'll help you. Promise!" She gulped and wiped the sleeve of her shirt over her eyes. "I'll put in a good word for you."

They glanced at each other again. One of them started to speak, but the other one roughly elbowed him into silence. Dallas motioned behind her back for one of her classmates to step forward and separate the two men. She silently prayed they would take her cue and play bad cop so she could continue playing the good cop.

Haliburton sauntered over. "Alright, let's go." He reached for the shoulders of the guy who wasn't cooperating. "Told you these guys weren't going to be any help to us, officer. Not sure why you're wasting your time with them."

"No, please. Wait!" Dallas reached for the arm of the guy who'd started to speak. "This one wants to help us find Mary. He understands how much danger she's in, because he has a kid sister. Isn't that right?" She stared straight into his face, allowing more large crocodile tears to roll down her cheeks.

He nodded again.

"Please help me find her before it's too late. I'll do everything I can to help you in return."

He ducked his head and muttered, "He left her in the freezer in the storage room."

Though her heart sank at the knowledge that the child was likely no longer alive, Dallas whirled around to face her classmates. "Where's the storage room?"

Instructor Ryker, who hadn't spoken a word during the last few hours, pushed away from the wall and clapped his hands. "Congratulations. You just cracked the case and found the missing girl." He dug in the pocket of his safety vest and came up with a travel pack of tissues. "Nice acting, Officer Hill. Looks like there's plenty of room for your Hollywood skills in law enforcement. We're lucky you chose to join our ranks."

It was high praise coming from him, and they all knew it. "That was a textbook perfect interrogation. You established common ground with the perps, played on their emotions, and made a few nonspecific but compelling promises to scratch their backs if they scratched yours. Then you separated the witnesses when you saw one of them starting to crack. As for the rest of you." He spread his hands. "It was wise going to radio silence before you entered the building. Wise to work in pairs. Wise to give your dogs their heads and let them do what they're trained to do. Wise to clear the building before expanding your search. Officers riddled with bullets are a lot less effective than uninjured ones. Take a minute to congratulate each other for a job well done."

Realizing that meant they'd passed their final hurdle to graduate, Dallas's classmates erupted into cheers, hugs, and back slaps — kicking up no small amount of dust in the process.

Hunt watched them, arms folded, like a proud parent. "Now for the constructive criticism. What did you do wrong? What could you have done better? What will you do differently next time?"

"Check our equipment before leaving the staging area," Dallas groaned.

"Yep. No matter how experienced you get, you never outgrow the ABC's and 123's. What else?"

"After comparing notes, it appears all of our dogs lingered near the freezer," Haliburton offered with a rueful look. "I know we eventually found the girl, but the clock never stops ticking. Every minute she was in the freezer spelled the difference between the simple shivers, full-blown hypothermia, and eventual cardiac arrest."

"Exactly, sheriff. That's why we train as hard as we do."

The jarring sound of an amber alert blasted in unison across their respective radios and cell phones, which most of Dallas's classmates had turned on after the exercise was concluded.

"Is this part of the exercise?" One of the Evans twins elbowed his brother.

"I don't think so." His brother shook his head, looking worried.

"Me, neither." Sanchez raised his smart watch, his dark eyebrows raised. "Nothing like finding out a real crisis is going down a few miles from the training center, right after what we just experienced." He shook his head. "Makes me want to jump back inside the Batmobile and head across town to help out. What do you say, Instructor Ryker? Is that even allowed?" He wrinkled his forehead. "I know we don't graduate until tomorrow, but..."

Dallas glanced over at Hunt when he didn't respond and found him half turned away from them, speaking on his cell phone.

"Roger that, sir. I'm on my way." He turned back to them, his swarthy features set in grave lines. "I heard what you said, Trainee Sanchez, and the answer is yes. That's a real amber alert, and they could really use our help this afternoon over in Glen Rose. It's not mandatory, and your participation or lack thereof will not affect your final grade in the program. However, I'll gladly take any of you who wish to go get some real-life experience."

"Yo!" Sanchez waved a finger in the air and took a step forward. "Sign me up."

"I'm in." Haliburton didn't hesitate. He regarded Dallas with a mocking grin. "Well, officer, are you ready to call it a night?"

Before she could answer, Tracy Miller nervously twisted a finger through her ponytail. "Gosh, I hate to be the only party pooper here, but I promised the front office folks I'd stop by after class today to clear up a discrepancy in my file. I'd hate to miss graduating on some technicality."

One of the Evans twins grabbed two handfuls of red hair and groaned, "At least you have a valid excuse for ducking out. Ours is much lamer."

"Yeah," his brother snorted, "if it wouldn't cause World War III in the Evans clan, we'd be glad to join you. But..." he wrinkled his freckled nose, "four generations of Evanses are in the process of descending on this town, so family duty calls."

"No problem." Hunt's slate gaze rested on Dallas. "Like I said, class is over. What comes next is strictly voluntary."

"Well, Officer Hill," Haliburton taunted. "What's it gonna be? Beauty sleep, family duty, or work?"

Gosh, she so wasn't going to miss his smug face after tomorrow! "First of all," she pointed with both forefingers at her face, "this mug doesn't require extra sleep to be fabulous."

"Ooooo!" Sanchez sang out. "Bring out the sword, lady!"

"Secondly," she continued, turning sober, "the only family I have is behind bars, so my schedule is wide open." In fact, work might actually be the one thing that kept her from wallowing in self-pity the rest of the night while the families of her classmates continued pouring into town.

"Oh, man!" For the first time since they'd met,

Haliburton visibly deflated. "I had no idea. I, ah..." He dropped his arms and took an uncertain step toward her.

She waved a finger beneath his nose. "Stop right there, partner! One more step and Lady might decide to practice her newly acquired attack skills on you." She bent down to slide a hand across her dog's glossy black flanks. "Lucky for you, I'd rather save her secret sauce for the *really* bad guys."

He snorted and resumed his cocky stance. "Glad to know where I rank."

"You're welcome." She intended to shoot him a sassy grin but ended up meeting Hunt's gaze, instead.

What she read there nearly took her breath away — pure, unadulterated adoration. Then it was gone.

"Let's load up and head back to the staging area, shall we?" he announced, glancing around the room at her classmates. "It's going to be a long night for some of us."

His smoldering gaze returned to her as they made their way back to the vehicle.

CHAPTER 7: AMBER ALERT

HUNT

Sanchez hopped behind the wheel and started driving again, while Hunt dialed the cafeteria. "Hey, what are the chances of getting four boxed meals to go in the next fifteen to twenty minutes?" He paused to listen. "Yes, that would be perfect. I'll send someone down there to pick them up."

In less than five minutes, they were parked back at the staging area, which was much more crowded than when they'd left it. It looked as if the training center officials had opened it up for overflow parking. There were a few commercial vans and RVs lining the outer perimeter of the lot.

Haliburton whistled. "Looks like half of Texas has descended on us."

Hunt pushed open his door and leaped down from the passenger seat, flagging down an intern pushing an empty supply cart. "It's going to get a lot more crowded by morning. They've invited the attorney general to serve as the keynote speaker for your graduation."

"Bonus!" Dallas's gaze snapped with a new layer of interest. "I've heard he has an amazing story to tell about why he first decided to put on the blue."

Hunt nodded in agreement, wishing more than anything that she was his to hold and kiss already. He ached to have her soft, slender curves back in his arms and have all of that blue-eyed sparkle directed straight up at him. *Soon, baby, soon!* Instead, he dragged his gaze away from her to address the intern as the guy parked his cart next to the SUV.

"We have an order of boxed meals to pick up at the cafeteria, and I'd like a case of water bottles to go with it. Chilled, if possible, but we'll take whatever they have."

"Roger that, sir. I'll have your order filled within the hour."

"How about in the next ten to fifteen minutes?" Hunt glanced at his watch. "We're trying to make it to Glen Rose as soon as possible to help out with the amber alert."

"Shoot, yeah! I heard about that on the news. They've shut down the whole dinosaur park." The sandy-haired fellow took out his electronic pad and tapped something on the screen. "Tell you what, sir.

I'll have those boxed meals and waters back to you as soon as humanly possible."

"Can't ask for more than that." Hunt grinned his appreciation

The intern literally took off at a sprint across the parking lot, pushing his cart as if his life depended on it.

"This is a pretty special place, isn't it?" Dallas asked softly as she stared after him.

Hunt glanced her way, surprised to find her hovering near his elbow. It wasn't like her to stand this close to him in public. Or engage him in a personal conversation. Or address him at all, really. They'd made a habit of keeping their distance from each other during her entire stint at the Texas Hotline Training Center. Yet here they were, standing together behind the open doors of the SUV, facing the dog cages. Both PoPo and Lady were twitching and whining to be let out.

"Very special, I agree." Since Haliburton and Sanchez were both hustling their dogs across the parking lot to the kennel to be fed and watered, he risked adding, "Just for the record, I'm going to miss seeing you every day after tomorrow."

She blushed and glanced down at the latch on Lady's cage that she'd been fiddling with. "I'm going to miss you, too." Her voice was barely above a whisper.

"I plan to see what I can do to remedy that." After another glance around the crowded parking lot, he set his cell phone on the floor of the SUV in front of the dog cages and slid it her way. "Number, please."

His heart pounded as he watched her pink-tipped fingers type the digits. The name she added made him grin like a lovesick moron. She'd typed *The Real Dallas Hill.*

"I'm so glad I kissed the right girl," he muttered.

"Me, too." She unlatched Lady's cage. Since the parking lot was so jam-packed with people, she attached the dog's leash before allowing her to jump down to the ground.

Hunt did the same with PoPo. "Any chance I can talk you into having him fed and watered for me while I finish gathering our gear?"

A soft smile tugged at her lips. "No problem, Instructor Ryker." Then she added with a sassy glance up at him, "After graduation tomorrow, you'll probably be able to talk me into a few other things."

He caught his breath, unable to tear his gaze away from hers. "All I can say, Officer Hill, is it's a good thing we have work to do. I wouldn't be getting much sleep tonight, thinking about all the wonderful things that are going to happen tomorrow."

She gave a breathless laugh. "Got it that bad for me, huh?"

"And then some!" It took a superhuman effort to make himself lean away from her instead of closer. "Now get out of here before I kiss you again and get myself fired."

Her feminine laughter trilled around his ears as she jogged away. The sound of it warmed the coldest, loneliest parts of his heart. She was so perfect for him. Smart, wildly talented, brave, strong, and full of compassion for others. He was the luckiest guy on the planet to be the one she'd chosen to kiss nine months ago, nearly ten months ago now. No, it was more than luck. What felt like an accidental encounter at the beginning was something that was meant to be.

He returned his attention to assessing the gear in the back of the SUV, quickly assessing what needed to be restocked.

"She's pretty incredible, isn't she?"

Hunt stiffened at the sound of Jug Dawson's voice. He glanced over to find the guy standing near his elbow. "Didn't hear you approach, sir."

"Probably because I snuck up on you." The lead instructor pushed back his cap to lean inside the SUV. He rummaged curiously through the supplies. "Looks like you've got most of what you need already. Want me to ride along?"

Hunt shrugged. "That's entirely up to you, sir. You'll be pleased to know I have three student volunteers joining us — Sanchez, Haliburton, and Hill."

His boss snorted. "I think it's safe to say that one of us is more pleased than the other about the fact that Hill will be in attendance."

Hunt's head shot up. "Are you accusing me of something, Officer Dawson?"

"Nope. You're one of the finest instructors I've ever worked with." He ducked his head to stare at Hunt over his reading glasses. "Even though I never bought that I-kissed-her-double hogwash."

Hunt straightened his shoulders. "What do you mean? It was all over the news if you want to fact-check my story."

"Yeah, and I have eyes to see what's written all over your face, Ryker. You care for her."

"Is it that obvious?" Hunt shook his head in disgust. He'd tried really hard throughout the past month to conduct himself in a professional manner. No one in class could honestly claim he'd gone easy on Dallas. Jug Dawson had to have noticed that, so why was he choosing to make a big deal out of the situation the day before she graduated?

"To most people? No. To a man with a degree in kinesthetics? Clear as water."

"No kidding, sir! A degree in kinesthetics, huh?" Hunt's disgruntled mood swiftly faded into admiration.

"Yep. A master's degree. I'm very good at reading body language, Instructor Ryker, so you might as well shoot straight with me in the future."

In the future. Hunt slowly blew out the breath he'd been holding, liking the sound of the fact that he still had a job. "It was more a matter of omission."

"True dat."

"Would you have done anything differently if you were in my shoes? For real, sir?" Hunt watched his boss intently, truly wanting to know if the man thought he should have handled the situation differently.

"Probably not." Officer Dawson chuckled. "At least not in front of a student. You could have squared things away with me later on, though."

"In hindsight, I wish I had, sir." Hunt met the lead instructor's gaze steadily. Unfortunately, trust wasn't something a person could just dole out. Folks had to earn it. "If I knew you then as well as I do now, I would have."

"Glad to hear it." Jug Dawson glanced up as Sanchez and Haliburton jogged back in their direction. "I hope that means you plan to stick around for a while."

"It does, sir."

"Good." His boss thrust out a hand. "It looks like you and I have trained a solid team to lend a hand in Glen Rose tonight."

"The very best, sir," Hunt agreed. "Wish you could have observed them in action at the city rubble simulation earlier."

"Me, too." The lead instructor's voice was wry. "Unlike you, however, I'm forever getting dragged away to meetings and such. In fact, they're asking me to attend a dinner with the attorney general this evening." He arched his dark brows inquiringly at Hunt.

"We can handle Glen Rose, sir."

"If you're sure about it, I'm going to take you at your word."

"I'm sure, sir." Hunt appreciated the man's vote of confidence, especially considering that the mission would place Dallas Hill beneath his leadership once again.

"Then go find that kiddo and bring 'em home."

"That's the plan, sir." Hunt couldn't make any blanket promises in that direction, and he knew his boss didn't expect him to.

As Officer Dawson strode away, he passed the intern, who'd gone to fetch their box meals. He was rolling his cart noisily across the parking lot, keeping a hand on the tray of meals to steady them.

"That was quick," Hunt noted in satisfaction. "Do you accept tips?" He wasn't quite sure what the protocol was for stuff like that at the training center.

"So long as it's a high-five or a fist-bump, sir," the intern panted. He was out of breath from his mad dash to and from the cafeteria.

"How about a candy bar?" Sanchez arrived in

time to overhear what the intern said and tossed him a Snickers.

"Wow, thanks!" The intern caught it gleefully and doled out a round of fist bumps. Then he loaded up the case of water and box meals in the back of the SUV. "Hope you find the kid." He saluted them and took off with his empty cart.

"Where's Officer Hill?" Hunt demanded, impatiently scanning the parking lot behind his two students.

Haliburton tossed his thumb in the direction of the kennel. "Right behind us."

Hunt squinted through the sunlight to see Dallas hurrying their way with two dogs on leashes and something clasped under each arm.

He huffed out a chuckle to realize she was lugging four raincoats as she got closer. "Afraid of getting wet, Officer Hill?"

"Actually, I am, sir," she retorted. "According to the vet, we may be heading into a thunderstorm. Though this mug is bulletproof, as previously stated, both of my classmates can attest to the fact that I'm so sweet I might melt."

Haliburton groaned as he secured his Rottweiler in his cage. "Far be it from me to contradict a lady, but..." He curled his upper lip at her. "That's a load of bull." He jiggled the cage door to make sure it was locked. "You look sweet, but you ain't. You're a hard-as-nails police officer whose bad side I do not want to be on."

Hunt was surprised to hear Haliburton's assessment of Dallas. Unless he was missing something, it sounded like she'd finally won the guy over.

She glanced laughingly over at her classmate. "Thanks, I think." Then she reached for the first boxed meal and tossed it at Sanchez.

He caught it and bowed his head in a silent blessing before tearing it open and digging out his sandwich.

Hunt secured the doors behind the dogs. "Let's get this show on the road. I'll brief you about the case on the way there."

Dallas gathered up the rest of the boxed meals and climbed through the back passenger door with her arms full.

Haliburton slipped around Hunt and reached for the front passenger door. For a second, he thought the guy was actually going to open the door for him.

"Mind if I ride shotgun this time, sir?" Haliburton angled his head at Dallas. "It's an hour-long drive there, and it ain't exactly a secret that I'm not her favorite."

But that wasn't his real reason, and they both knew it. There'd been something different about the hot-headed sheriff ever since his last clash of horns with Dallas.

Haliburton motioned for him to step aside with him out of her earshot. Speaking in a low voice to Hunt, he confided, "Tracy, er, I mean Officer Miller told me that Officer Hill's mother is the family member who's in jail, sir."

Hunt stared at his student for a moment, hoping he'd heard wrong, but knowing he hadn't. What a bum deal Dallas had been landed with in the parent department! Though his gut wrenched with sympathy, he forced himself to maintain a bland expression, "And you're telling me this, because?"

Haliburton lifted his cap to run a hand through his short, spiky blonde hair. "I dunno, sir. I guess because Officer Miller said that's why it was so easy for Officer Hill to cry earlier during the simulation, and I'm no good at dealing with squishy stuff like that."

"Good gravy, sheriff!" Hunt choked back a laugh. "You did *not* just call one of your classmates squishy." Soft, curvy, and breathtakingly gorgeous, maybe, but not squishy, for crying out loud!

"Does that mean I can ride shotgun, sir?" His mouthiest student fixed him with a hopeful expression.

Hunt rolled his eyes and waved him aboard. If he was being honest with himself, spending the next hour in the back seat with Dallas wasn't exactly breaking his heart.

Her eyes widened as he slid onto the seat cushion next to her. Then they grew soft. However, her voice was complaining as she exclaimed, "Aw, you just ruined my reputation, Haliburton! Now everyone is going to accuse me of being the teacher's pet!"

"Negatory," Sanchez sang out from the front seat. "That spot is already solidly taken by your faithful chauffeur. Right, sir?"

"Just drive," Hunt retorted dryly, but it made him feel good that his team had developed such a solid rapport. It pleased him even more to know that it hadn't grown out of anything less than honest-to-gosh rigorous training and hard work. Dallas and her classmates had sweated together, suffered together, and developed into skilled search and rescue professionals together. He was enormously proud of all six of them.

As their team rolled from the parking lot, Dallas handed out the rest of the boxed meals. Hunt quickly discovered he was hungry enough to inhale everything their chef had prepared and even considered gnawing on the empty box afterward.

Eyeing his empty sandwich wrapper, Dallas held out the second half of her own sandwich. "You want it, sir? I cheated and had a granola bar earlier."

Sanchez made a growling sound. "You trying to horn in on my spot as teacher's pet back there?"

"Weren't you told to shut up and drive?" she shot back.

Too hungry to negotiate, Hunt quickly polished off her sandwich and washed it down with half a bottle of water. Feeling fueled up, he leaned forward conversationally in his seat, resting his forearms on his knees. "So here's the low-down on the case. A five-month-old boy named Jackson went missing around eleven-thirty this morning at the Dinosaur Valley State Park."

"Only five-months-old?" Dallas looked stricken.

"Most unfortunately." The way she paled made him long to reach out and lace his fingers through hers, but he resisted the temptation. She wasn't his to hold yet. Not for another whole day. "Every child abduction is unfortunate, but when there's a baby involved, it's even harder."

"That's just sick," Sanchez snarled, gripping the steering wheel harder.

"Yeah," Hunt sighed, "and it's one of those small towns where everybody knows everybody, so folks are pretty broken up about it."

"Any suspects?" Haliburton sounded equally furious.

"Nothing solid yet. Jane Smith is a single mother who works as a waitress at a local diner. Showed up a few months ago with a baby in her arms. No father in the picture, at least not one she's willing to talk about. It's one of those everybody-loves-her situations, though nobody seems to know much about her."

Haliburton whistled. "Jane Smith. That doesn't sound made up at all."

"Agreed." Hunt liked his student's quick thinking. "Everyone the sheriff has interviewed brags up a storm about how perfectly she mixes their coffee and how she remembers everyone's names and orders. But they can't tell you much else about her."

Sanchez made a clucking sound. "One of those people who talks a lot and says nothing about themselves. Nope. Like Haliburton said, nothing to hide there."

"Descriptions, please," Dallas interjected.

"Mother is blonde, late twenties, and runs about five miles per day, according to the landlord who babysits for her. The kid is mixed. Half white, half black. Sheriff seems to think there's some Caribbean blood in him, but he's not a hundred percent sure."

"Sounds like the mother is a lot of help," Sanchez noted dryly.

"Ah, cut her some slack," Dallas muttered. "If she blew into town under a fake name, she probably had her reasons. For all we know, we're dealing with a battered woman, which would easily explain her reluctance to talk about her past."

"That's one theory, anyway." Hunt liked how the combined curiosity and logic of his team were coming together. He'd only given them a few details, and they were already gnawing their way through the likeliest scenarios. He especially liked how Dallas so sweetly and effortlessly offered the insight of a woman to the otherwise all-male conversation.

The hour-long drive passed quickly. They arrived at a set of entrance gates flanked by an enormous pair of fiberglass dinosaurs — one in the shape of an Apatosauras and the other in the shape of a Tyrannosaurus Rex. Cars were jammed like sardines in the parking lot, many of them bearing license plates from other counties. Hunt wasn't surprised by the amount of help pouring in. A missing baby had a way of doing that.

Hunt and his team were pointed toward a section of forest to canvas along the Paluxy River. "We've been at it for hours, but there's still a lot of ground to cover. Too much ground." The sheriff stood with Hunt and his students outside the main museum building, greeting newcomers and assigning tasks as quickly as they arrived.

He lifted his Stetson and repositioned it on his graying hair as he sized up Hunt's team. They stood in a semi-circle around him, silently absorbing everything they were being told. "The park grounds alone span more than 1,500 acres." Worry lines creased the edges of the man's eyes. "We've barricaded all entrances and exits. There are patrols on the perimeter and a few boats on the river, but..." He shook his head.

Hunt understood what he'd left unsaid. There was no easy way to secure that much real estate. The kidnapper or kidnappers might be long gone by now. A drone of helicopters overhead alerted him to the fact they had air support, as well.

"Here's a photograph of the little tyke." The sheriff's voice cracked hoarsely as he handed over a full-color eight-by-ten of the missing child.

Hunt stood riveted as he stared at the photograph. He blinked a few times to clear his vision and looked again. And found himself staring at a miniature version of none other than Marcus Zane! His heart thumped so crazily in his chest that he had to drag in several short, uneven breaths before speaking again.

He canted his head at the sheriff. "Any chance I can speak with the mother real quick?"

The man frowned thoughtfully. "As you can imagine, she's pretty distraught, so we've tried to shield her from—"

"I think I may know something about the child's father." As insane as his theory was, Hunt knew he was onto something. He needed to speak with the missing kid's mother. Now. His sense of urgency grew with each passing second.

The sheriff sized him up again before capitulating. "Ah, what the heck? Why not?" He eyed the rest of Hunt's team. "I'm sending you in alone, though, so as not to overwhelm her."

Sanchez scorched Hunt with a searching look as the sheriff escorted their team toward the entrance of the building. "Anything you want to fill us in on, boss man?"

"Probably." Hunt's blood pounded against his temples. "But I need to speak to Jane Smith first to be sure. Then we'll talk."

As if sensing something monumental was taking place, Haliburton reached out to clap him on the shoulder. Dallas stepped closer and managed to brush the outside of his hand with her fingertips. It was a small, subtle gesture, but it was enough to buoy his strength to deal with what was coming next.

Where are you, Marcus? Why is there a missing kid out there who looks just like you?

The woman waiting inside the museum was the anti-thesis of what the sheriff had described. She was no weeping, swooning damsel in distress. Not even close. She swung around at the sound of the door opening, her brown eyes spitting fire.

"I should be out there looking for my son," she snapped, white-faced. "I don't know why you insist on keeping me holed up like a rat in a trap." Her gaze slid around the sheriff's paunchy figure and landed on Hunt. "You!" she breathed and paled another several degrees.

"Do you know each other?" The sheriff's head swiveled between the two of them.

"Yes," she snarled.

"No," Hunt said at the same time. "We only met once," he amended lamely. It had been at a checkpoint in Afghanistan. Marcus had managed to get her phone number and had promised to call her upon his return to the states. From the looks of things, he'd made that call and then some!

"Would either of you mind telling me what's going on?" The sheriff's voice was beseeching.

"Actually, I'd like to speak with Staff Sergeant Ryker alone," the woman retorted, never taking her eyes off of Hunt.

"Are you sure that's wise, ma'am?" The middle-aged lawman made a spluttering sound of protest. "I mean—"

"Oh, for crying out loud, sheriff!" she exploded. "He's a bloody war hero with a bloody Purple Heart. I'm safer with him than half the morons you've got running around outside like chickens with their heads cut off."

"Yes, ma'am." Hunt inwardly snickered at the way the man threw his hands up in defense and backed swiftly from the room. The moment the door shut behind him, Jane Smith stalked forward.

"It's about time you made your appearance, Hunt Ryker, especially since there's a good chance this is all your fault!"

His jaw dropped. *What did I ever do to you, lady?*

She marched right up to him and waved her finger beneath his nose. "Poking around in things that don't concern you, snapping satellite photos, and asking stupid questions." Her voice gathered steam. "Naturally, my husband's enemies came looking for him, which led them straight to me and Jackson."

Hunt had no idea who *they* were, or what dangers the young wife was referring to. His half-numb brain had latched on to one detail only.

For a moment, exhilaration flooded his chest, rocking him so powerfully that it was difficult to breathe. "Marcus is alive, isn't he?" He shook his head in amazement and added beneath his breath, "No wonder Jackson looks just like him!"

Jane Smith's dark gaze snapped with fury. "No thanks to you!"

His eyes grew damp at her confession. Not entirely sure what she was accusing him of, he exclaimed, "I knew it!"

"You crazy Marine!" Eyes filling, she threw her arms around him and buried her face against his chest. "You really should have left well enough alone. Just being in the same room with me is putting you in more danger than you can imagine."

It took a minute or two for Hunt to collect himself enough to question her.

"What danger?"

"I'm not at liberty to say." Her voice was muffled against his uniform.

Not helpful. He raised and lowered his hands

back to her shoulders. "Are you still serving in the Marines?"

She pulled away abruptly, wiping the backs of her hands across her eyes. "You're joking, right? I've been living in the middle of nowhere for the past six months, calling myself Jane Smith."

"Why?" He used the sleeve of his uniform to wipe his own eyes. "What's Marcus gotten himself mixed up with? The mafia?" Man, but he had a thousand questions to pummel the guy with the next time he saw him.

"As if," she snorted. "More like black ops."

Whoa! "I have so many questions I don't even know where to begin," he admitted, feeling dazed.

"Then don't." She started pacing the room again. "The less you know, the better. Trust me."

Well, too bad! His curiosity wasn't even close to being satisfied. "I take it you two are married now?"

"I said not to ask questions."

"Really?" He gaped at her. "You expect me to help you find your missing son, no questions asked?" As the old saying went, the magic was in the details.

"Yes. That's exactly what I need you to do."

He locked his hands behind his head and stared at her, perplexed. "I have a better idea. Why don't you simply tell me what you can, and we'll take it from there?"

She gave him a hard look. "Did you come alone?"

"No. I have three SAR trainees with me and four K9 search and rescue dogs."

"Babies!" she scoffed.

"They're actually pretty good at what they do." He folded his arms and held her gaze evenly. "I trained these students myself," he bragged. "They'll graduate tomorrow."

"Fine. Bring them in. If a Marine whipped them into shape, they're probably going to be more useful than all the others out there put together."

Not only did Hunt appreciate her matter-of-fact assessment of his abilities, he happened to agree with her. Whatever crooked path her and Marcus's lives had taken, they were still loyal to the Corps. That was a good sign.

Hunt took that moment to retrieve his team and bring them inside to meet with Jane Smith. He couldn't recall her real name, but that no longer seemed to matter.

Dallas took one look at his face and moved defensively to his side. "Are you okay?" she implored in a whisper.

He grimaced and whispered back, "I will be after we locate Jackson." Then he raised his voice so the rest of their team could hear him again.

"First of all, there will be no questions from any of you, and no communicating what you hear inside this building with anyone outside this building. Understood?"

"Roger that." Haliburton waved two fingers, looking intensely curious.

Sanchez's nod was a little slower to come, and Dallas didn't bother answering at all.

"Jackson was taken by someone or a group of someones to use as bait to draw his father out of hiding." That wasn't completely true, but it was close enough. "The good news is, they'll keep the kid alive."

"For now," Jane snapped. "I assure you, time is still vitally important." She glared at Hunt's team members one by one. "The men who took my son aren't near as dangerous as the ones they'll send next. At the moment, I suspect we're dealing with regular hitmen."

"Just a few paid hitmen," Sanchez interjected sarcastically. "No problem, ma'am. We'll just pull out our sniper guns and...oh, wait a sec!" He slapped a hand to his forehead. "We're not snipers. We're a regular ol' search and rescue squad!"

"Put a lid on it, Sanchez." Haliburton lightly punched his classmate's shoulder. "We're all lawmen here. And women." He pretended to curtsy to Dallas, making her smile. "Men and women who happen to know how to track down and disarm the enemy, thanks to Instructor Ryker."

"Just to be clear, this is a catch and release operation," Jane declared flatly, making a canceling motion with both hands. "The men who took my son cannot be brought in by the authorities for questioning under any circumstances. Just bring my son back to me, and we'll be gone by nightfall."

Sanchez made a silent O with his mouth and reached up to scratch his head. Glancing over at Hunt, he demanded, "So what are our marching orders, boss man?"

"Bullet-proof vests for us and muzzles for our dogs. Can't have them giving away our position with a bunch of barking." He turned to Jane. "Should we start our search inside the park or outside the park?"

She shrugged. "As crazy as it sounds, my gut says to start inside. I'll show you the spot where my baby was snatched." She tapped a finger against her chin. "They're probably under orders to stay in town, because they'll need a set of coordinate points to draw my son's father out of hiding. They'll keep moving, too, because of all the search teams on the ground, but they won't go far. They'll circle the area to confuse the dogs and maybe cross the river to confuse the trail."

Dallas scowled at her. "Or, better yet, they'll hide in plain sight."

Everyone turned to stare at her.

"I'm listening, if you have a theory to share," Hunt assured coolly. His instincts told him she was working on one.

"If I had to hide a baby with this many SAR teams crawling the grounds, I'd pose as a set of rescue workers. Because of the dogs, I'd stick to the edge of the crowd and pretty much do what you said. Circle, cross the river, rinse, and repeat."

Jane nodded in approval. "She'd make a good Marine, Ryker."

"I was thinking the same thing." If it was one day later, he would've shamelessly kissed his woman right then and there in front of them all. Instead, he grinned at his team and gloated, "Officer Hill's theory makes perfect sense, so let's suit up and go rescue that baby."

IN THE END, they opted to wait until nightfall, when the volunteers thinned out and started to trickle home. Hunt and his team donned their bullet-proof vests and heat sensor goggles. Then they muzzled the dogs and made their way to the site of the kidnapping. It was located deep inside the park.

Against the sheriff's loud and vociferous protests, Jane insisted on suiting up and joining them. He was following standard protocols by keeping the parent nearby for when the missing child was found. He had no idea that Jane planned on ditching Glen Rose the moment Jackson was returned to her.

"Here," Jane whispered, pointing at the spot. According to her story on the hike there, she'd been standing barefoot on the dry edge of the riverbed.

Her baby had been strapped to her chest inside a cloth carrier. She'd been approached from behind, rendered unconscious with a chemical-soaked cloth, and stripped of her precious burden.

"Radio silence," Hunt ordered tersely. He and his students gave their dogs a minute or so to bury their noses in one of Jackson's onesies. Then the creatures began to sniff their way around the riverbed. Next, Hunt split their group into two teams. Sanchez and Haliburton took one side of the river. He, Dallas, and Jane took the other side.

In less than thirty minutes, they found their marks. A pair of men were camped at the edge of the river beside a small tent. According to Hunt's heat vision goggles, there was a much tinier human resting inside the tent.

Since Jane wanted them to take no prisoners, Hunt knew what he had to do. His team would be forced to observe from the sidelines and take it as a teachable moment, because the rest of the mission was going to require a Marine.

He briefly explained to Sanchez, Haliburton, and Dallas that he needed them and Jane to continue circling with the dogs, pretending to search for the missing baby. Not only would it keep a sense of normalcy about their movements, it would ultimately keep them safe from the kidnappers. It would additionally provide a much-needed distraction for what he was going to do next.

"Take off the muzzles," he commanded, "and let the dogs bark. Be clunky and noisy like amateurs, but don't overdo it. Most importantly, keep your distance from the kidnappers."

"How far back should we stay?" Dallas studied him with worry.

"Out of shooting range."

She sucked in a breath. "You're going after them alone, aren't you?"

He held her gaze and answered with his eyes instead of using words.

She shooed her classmates away. "Go! I'll catch up." The second they were out of earshot, she tugged on Hunt's hand. "I have one last thing to say before you do this."

She paused and glanced pointedly in Jane's direction. The young mother reached knowingly for the leashes of the two remaining dogs and moseyed after Sanchez and Haliburton.

Dallas quickly backed toward a copse of trees, tugging Hunt with her.

"What are you doing?" *Oh!* He lost all power of speech when she slid her arms around his neck and pressed her lips to his.

He cuddled her close and eagerly returned her kiss, reveling in the sweetness of being claimed by her at long last. He never wanted to let her go, though he knew he had to.

"I love you, Hunt Ryker," she whispered against

his lips.

Her words rendered him momentarily inco-
herent with joy, so he did the next best thing. He
dove in for another soul-shattering kiss.

She ended it way too soon. Lightly shoving at his
chest, she declared, "Go get that baby! Then come
back to me in one piece."

"Yes, ma'am!" Before he lost his resolve to leave
the woman of his dreams, he dropped to his belly
and low-crawled his way in the direction of the tent.

The mission grew tense when one of the men
abruptly stood up and started walking in his direction. At first, he feared his position had been compro-
mised, but it turned out the kidnapper was only
answering the call of nature. Hunt silently crept up
behind him and put him in a chokehold. Though the
thug wrestled viciously for air, Hunt had the advan-
tage of surprise and dropped him noiselessly to the
ground.

To his amusement, the fellow was wearing a
black ski mask. *Too easy.* He yanked it off and pulled
it over his own face. Knowing he didn't have long
before the man awoke, he walked straight up to the
other guy. By the time the poor sap realized Hunt
wasn't the person he was expecting, it was too late. A
well-placed punch rendered him as senseless as his
partner.

Hunt quickly retrieved the sleeping Jackson

from inside the tent and took off running with him tucked under his arm like a football.

He met his team and Jane at the river's edge.

She gave a shaky sob and reached for Jackson. "*Semper Fi*, Hunt. I'll never forget this."

"*Simper Fi*, Jane." He snapped out a quick salute.

Then she was gone.

CHAPTER 8: GRADUATION

DALLAS

Before Dallas and her classmates reached the SUV, a crack of thunder splintered the air, and the sky opened up. They were drenched by the time they climbed aboard. So were their dogs.

Sanchez started the ignition with a shiver. He turned on the heater and soon had such hot air blasting into the cab that Haliburton threatened to fire him as their driver.

"Suck it up, buttercup," Sanchez quavered through chattering teeth. "I'm just a skinny dude. I don't have your kinda meat on my bones." However, he turned the heat down to less of an inferno.

Dallas fumbled damply with the latches on the cages in the back, loading up all four dogs. She tucked spare towels and blankets around each of them and gave them milk bones for a job well done. "You wonderful beasts," she crooned. "Good job!"

She received a few licks in return, which she didn't mind one bit.

To her enormous relief, Hunt rejoined them minutes later. "Well, the sheriff wasn't too thrilled to hear it, but I told him the perps abandoned the baby near the river. He was even less thrilled to learn his mama snatched him up and fled town. I'll probably get called back for another round of questioning, but there's not much he can do other than close the case."

"What case?" Haliburton drawled. "All I did was spend an evening walking my dog around the Dinosaur Valley Park. And the worse part about it? I didn't see any dinosaurs."

Sanchez nodded. "Just for the record, my dog and I are equally disappointed. All we got was soaked."

Dallas tossed one of the rain coats over her shoulders and snuggled beneath it. "Well, I didn't see any dinosaurs, either, but I got kissed by three fabulous guys."

"What?" Sanchez and Haliburton cried in unison, heads whipping around to ogle her.

She counted them off on her fingers. "Well, there was PoPo, for starters, then a certain chocolate-colored Rottweiler named Bruiser, then..." She ducked when Sanchez wadded up his empty sandwich wrapper and sent it zooming into the back seat.

Hunt snapped out a hand and caught it.

"My hero," she murmured sleepily. Heavens, but she was wildly tempted to scoot over a few inches to rest her head against his shoulder. *Tomorrow,* she promised herself.

SHE WOKE the next morning to a rainstorm pounding against the roof and windows of the women's dormitory. "Really?" She groaned as she threw back the blankets and crawled barefoot out of bed. "After all we've endured the past month, we have to graduate in this?"

"You were out awfully late last night," Tracy teased as they donned their black cargo uniforms for the last time.

"Oh, you haven't heard the best part yet." Dallas waggled her eyebrows at her friend. "I got kissed by three different guys." At Tracy's gasp and the barrage of questions that followed, she flipped on her phone and displayed a selfie of her being half-mauled by PoPo.

"Oh, please!" Tracy waved a hand in disappointment. "Call me when you've got a real story, sister." She pulled out a compact mirror and rolled on a layer of sparkly pink lip gloss. Then she made a few loud smacking sounds before popping the lid back on the tube.

Dallas finished French braiding her hair and

tucked it under her cap. *Girl, you have no idea the stories I could tell you from last night!* "So what was up with your file?"

"Oh, nothing." Tracy waved a hand airily. "I just didn't want to spend a minute longer than necessary in our stuffy instructor's presence."

Dallas's jaw dropped in shock. "Instructor Ryker? How could you say such a thing about him? He's so—"

"Gotcha!" her friend chortled, shaking a finger at her. "I actually have nothing against him. I just wanted to see how hard you would blush and how quickly you would jump to his defense."

"Tracy!" she protested, trying to look innocent.

"Spare me, sweetie." The woman rolled her eyes. "Just invite me to the wedding, and I'll promise to invite you to mine and Haliburton's in return."

"You and Haliburton?" Dallas held up a hand. "No. I can't go there. I just can't."

"Aw, he's not that bad!"

"I love you, Tracy, but that man is the spawn of Satan. Please, please, please tell me you're joking about marrying him!"

"No can do." The tall blonde batted her lashes as they exited the dormitory. "Oh, and be sure to congratulate him on our engagement. He still thinks it's a secret, though I've told half the class already."

"When did this happen?" Dallas shook her head in disbelief.

"Don't look at me like that." Tracy shot her an innocent look. "You're equally guilty of canoodling your way through our training."

"I have no idea what you're talking about!" Blushing harder than ever, Dallas shrugged on her rain jacket.

"Oh, but you do, darling!" Laughing, Tracy dashed at her side the short distance to the auditorium.

Haliburton and Sanchez beckoned them to the second row. Apparently, the two guys had been saving seats for their entire team.

Dallas folded her rain jacket and placed it beneath her chair. "I hear you're engaged, Haliburton." She forced a smile. "I don't know how you fooled Tracy into thinking you were from the human race, but somehow you did it. Congratulations."

"Engaged?" Haliburton looked down his nose at her and gave her one of his superior smiles. "I was engaged a long time ago, Officer Hill. I'm a married man now." With a lazy grin, he leaned across the seat to seal his mouth over Tracy's.

Sanchez cocked one brow in puzzlement. Then his eyes bugged out when Haliburton deepened the kiss. "You know what? I'm a single guy, so I'm just going to enjoy the show."

"Man, I've missed you!" Haliburton muttered to his wife when he raised his head.

Sanchez shook his head in disbelief. "Still not gonna ask."

Tracy smiled dreamily up at the man that Dallas couldn't imagine any woman being married to. "We were worried the training center wouldn't allow us into the same class if they knew we were married, so we ah... Well, let's just say that's the part of my file I had to clear up yesterday evening."

Dallas dissolved into giggles. She couldn't help it. "All those awful things I said about you, Haliburton." Her shoulders shook. "Which you richly deserved, if I may point out. To think that I was beefing to your wife all that time, though!"

"Devil's spa-a-awn!" he rasped in a stage whisper, making such a comical face that she laughed harder.

"Attention!"

The hubbub around them suddenly dimmed.

Dallas's class shot to their feet, arms fisted at their sides, faces staring straight ahead as their instructors marched onto the stage.

The last bubble of laughter died in her throat as Hunt Ryker made a perfect ninety-degree turn and faced her. His gaze sought her out and locked on hers.

My Marine. Dallas drank in his tall good looks, his strength, and the way he was kissing her with his eyes.

"Don't forget to invite us to the wedding," Tracy whispered.

Dallas blushed but didn't drop Hunt's gaze. This was their day. They'd waited so long for it.

The commander of the school moved to stand behind the podium. "It is my greatest pleasure to welcome the family, friends, and honored guests of the newest graduating class of the renowned Texas Hotline Training Center."

A thunderous applause broke out across the auditorium.

Though Dallas was thrilled to be graduating, she couldn't wait for the ceremony to be over. She barely heard a word of the keynote address she'd spent the last several weeks looking forward to. The highlight of the ceremony, by far, was when she walked across the stage.

Instructor Ryker handed over her diploma in a sealed envelope. "Congratulations, Officer Hill." As he shook her hand, his thumb intimately brushed across the inside of her palm.

It wasn't until she returned to her seat that she realized there was an extra sheet of paper tucked next to her diploma. It was the printout of a job listing for a position at the Glen Rose Police Department. Dallas's lips parted in wonder. Was this Hunt's way of asking her to stay in town?

The ceremony ended, and her classmates sent up a noisy cheer of victory. It was followed by a mass toss of their black caps into the air. Cameras flashed, and students lingered to pose with their favorite instructors. Then the crowd ventured outside to their waiting vehicles to head to celebratory parties and brunches.

The rain had finally stopped, and the sun was spilling out from behind the clouds. People gasped and pointed at a rainbow forming over the main lake behind the auditorium. More cameras flashed to catch the beauteous moment.

Feeling a bit melancholy over the fact that one of the most amazing month's of her life was over, Dallas slowed her steps as she headed toward her dormitory. As far as she could tell, she was the only person in her graduating class that had no family to celebrate the special occasion with.

A rumble of a helicopter overhead had her squinting upward. She stood back as a glossy white aircraft landed in the nearly empty dormitory parking lot.

A man leaned out of the cockpit and beckoned her forward.

Hunt? She blinked at him in surprise. Then she ducked beneath the whirling blades and ran to the door he was holding open. He reached down with one arm to scoop her inside.

"Congratulations on your graduation, Dallas." He tenderly brushed his lips over hers. "I'm so proud of you."

"Thank you." She gazed up at him with a full heart, realizing how wrong she'd been. She *did* have someone to celebrate this special day with, someone very much worth celebrating it with.

She glanced around them and gave a bounce of excitement. "This is so amazing!"

"You can thank my friend, Axel, when you meet him. He let me borrow the chopper."

"I didn't even know you had a pilot's license!"

He reached for her hand and raised it to his lips. "There are a lot of things you don't know about me, sweetheart, but I intend for that to change."

Her smile dimmed as she recalled the missing baby he'd fought so hard to recover, only to watch the mother disappear with him. "I'm sure there are things about your time in the Marines you probably can't talk about—"

"I was planning on telling you everything, " he assured "Don't want anything standing between me and the woman I love."

"Hunt," she breathed. She knew he cared about her, but it was the first time he'd actually said the words.

"And by love, I mean I'm head over heels in love with you, Dallas Hill."

Happiness filled her heart to the overflowing point. "Right back atcha, Marine." She reached up to touch his cheek.

He turned his head to kiss her fingers. "If you

don't already have plans, I'd like to take you somewhere and show you something."

"You're my plan, Hunt." It was the truth. She'd
never felt this way about anyone before.

"And you are mine — today, tomorrow, and the
next day." He leaned in for another lingering kiss.

"So what do you want to show me?" When he
lifted his head to gaze deeply into her eyes, she
studied him dreamily.

"An excellent question! I want to give you the
bird's-eye view of just how close Glen Rose is to the
training center." His thumb caressed her lower lip.
"In case you decide you can't bear the thought of
living too far away from me."

"Is this your way of saying you want me within
dating distance?"

"For a short time, yes." He bent to kiss her again,
taking his time and pouring his deepest longings into
it. "But I actually had something a little more permanent in mind."

"Hunt!" she gasped.

"What? Too soon?" He nuzzled the corner of her
mouth.

"No," she whispered. The timing felt just right
— absolutely perfect, in fact.

He chuckled. "I hope you were serious about
that, because I think you just agreed to marry me."

"I believe I did, Hunt Ryker." She blinked back

happy tears. It was the most wonderful feeling to realize she was no longer alone in the world.

Grinning joyfully, he throttled the engine and lifted the helicopter into the air. He circled the training center grounds at first, giving her a new perspective of the areas where they'd spent in so many grueling hours in recent days. The lakes were spectacular from this angle, with the sunlight glinting like hidden gems beneath the surface of the water.

Then he angled the aircraft and set their course for Glen Rose and the future they would build together.

Like this book? Leave a review now!

Join Jo's List and never miss a new release or a great sale on her books.

Want to read more about the missing Marcus Zane, little Jackson, and the woman who owns his heart — no matter how many miles are between them? Keep reading for a sneak peek of **THE BRIDESMAID RESCUE***!*

Much love,
Jo

SNEAK PREVIEW: THE BRIDESMAID RESCUE

A missing Marine, the woman he swears to call when he makes it safely home, and the wedding disaster that just might lead to a happily-ever-after no one saw coming...

Marcus Zane meets "the one" at a supply point before his Marine unit advances into enemy territory. He memorizes her phone number and promises to call her the day they return stateside. But a surprise attack leaves him missing in action, delaying his chance to keep his promise.

Emma Taylor has never been a wait-by-the-phone kind of girl, but it's love at first sight with the swoon-worthy Marine she meets overseas. So when he goes missing, she decides true love is worth waiting for — even if it means wearing a thousand

and one bridesmaid dresses before it's her turn to be a bride!

———

Grab your copy in eBook, paperback, or Kindle Unlimited on Amazon!
The Bridesmaid Rescue

Read them all!
The Plus One Rescue
The Secret Baby Rescue
The Bridesmaid Rescue
The Girl Next Door Rescue
The Secret Crush Rescue
The Bachelorette Rescue
The Rebound One Rescue
The Fake Bride Rescue
The Blind Date Rescue
The Maid by Mistake Rescue
The Unlucky Bride Rescue
The Temporary Family Rescue *— coming December, 2022!*

Much love,
Jo

NOTE FROM JO

Guess what? There's more going on in the lives of the hunky heroes you meet in my stories.

Because...*drum roll*...I have some Bonus Content for

everyone who signs up for my mailing list. From now on, there will be a special bonus content for each new book I write, just for my subscribers. Also, you'll hear about my next new book as soon as it's out (*plus you get a free book in the meantime*). Woohoo!

As always, thank you for reading and loving my books!

JOIN CUPPA JO READERS!

If you're on Facebook, please join my group, Cuppa Jo Readers. Don't miss out on the giveaways + all the sweet and swoony cowboys!

https://www.facebook.com/groups/ CuppaJoReaders

A scarred cowboy determined to remain single and the klutzy new ranch hand who trips up his carefully laid plans.

Asher Cassidy doesn't see himself getting hitched at a big church wedding anytime soon. Make that never. The freak fire that scarred one side of his face is a one-way ticket out of the dating game — something his interfering relatives don't seem to understand. Their endless matchmaking attempts keep him in a cranky mood.

He hires Bella Johnson as a ranch hand because she's so desperate for money that she'll have no choice but to put up with his grumpiness, the dirtiest chores, and whatever else he chooses to assign her. By some miracle, she even agrees to pose as his fake girlfriend at an upcoming hoedown, where his family plans to dangle him in front of yet more single ladies.

Sensing her new boss's gruff exterior is hiding a heart as broken as her own, Bella works extra hard to please him...or at least not get fired for her many mistakes while tackling her new job. Her biggest mistake of all turns out to be serving as his fake girlfriend. After tripping and falling into the cocky, sarcastic cowboy a half dozen or so times, she discovers that she enjoys being in his arms a little too much.

A sweet and inspirational, small-town romance with a few Texas-sized detours into comedy!

Hope you enjoyed the sneak preview of
COWBOY CONFESSIONS #1: Mr. Not Right for Her
Available in eBook, paperback, and hard cover on Amazon + FREE in Kindle Unlimited!

Read them all!
Mr. Not Right for Her
Mr. Maybe Right for Her

Much love,
Jo

SNEAK PREVIEW: HER BILLIONAIRE BOSS

Jacey Maddox didn't bother straightening her navy pencil skirt or smoothing her hand over the sleek lines of her creamy silk blouse. She already knew she looked her best. She knew her makeup was flawless, each dash of color accentuating her sun kissed skin and classical features. She knew this, because she'd spent way too many of her twenty-five years facing the paparazzi; and after her trust fund had run dry, posing for an occasional glossy centerfold — something she wasn't entirely proud of.

Unfortunately, not one drop of that experience lent her any confidence as she mounted the cold, marble stairs of Genesis & Sons. It towered more than twenty stories over the Alaskan Gulf waters, a stalwart high-rise of white and gray stone with tinted windows, a fortress that housed one of the world's most brilliant think tanks. For generations, the sons of Genesis had ridden the cutting edge of industrial design, developing the concepts behind some of the nation's most profitable inventions, products, and manufacturing processes.

It was the one place on earth she was least welcome.

Not just because of how many of her escapades had hit the presses during her rebel teen years. Not just because she'd possessed the audacity to marry their youngest son against their wishes. Not just because she had encouraged him to pursue his dreams instead of their hallowed corporate mission — a decision that had ultimately gotten him killed. No. The biggest reason Genesis & Sons hated her was because of her last name. The one piece of herself she'd refused to give up when she'd married Easton Calcagni.

Maddox.

The name might as well have been stamped across her forehead like the mark of the beast, as she moved into the crosshairs of their first security camera. It flashed an intermittent red warning light and gave a low electronic whirring sound as it swiveled to direct its lens on her.

Her palms grew damp and her breathing quickened as she stepped into the entry foyer of her family's greatest corporate rival.

Recessed mahogany panels lined the walls above a mosaic tiled floor, and an intricately carved booth anchored the center of the room. A woman with silver hair waving past her shoulders lowered her reading glasses to dangle from a pearlized chain. "May I help you?"

Jacey's heartbeat stuttered and resumed at a much faster pace. The woman was no ordinary receptionist. Her arresting blue gaze and porcelain features had graced the tabloids for years. She was Waverly, matriarch of the Calcagni family, grandmother to the three surviving Calcagni brothers. She was the one who'd voiced the greatest protests to Easton's elopement. She'd also wept in silence throughout his interment into the family mausoleum, while Jacey had stood at the edge of their gathering, dry-eyed and numb of soul behind a lacy veil.

The funeral had taken place exactly two months earlier.

"I have a one o'clock appointment with Mr. Luca Calcagni."

Waverly's gaze narrowed to twin icy points. "Not just any appointment, Ms. Maddox. You are here for an interview, I believe?"

Time to don her boxing gloves. "Yes." She could feel the veins pulsing through her temples now. She'd prepared for a rigorous cross-examination but had not expected it to begin in the entry foyer.

"Why are you really here?"

Five simple words, yet they carried the force of a full frontal attack. Beneath the myriad of accusations shooting from Waverly's eyes, she wanted to spin on her peep-toe stiletto pumps and run. Instead, she focused on regulating her breathing. It was a fair question. Her late husband's laughing face swam before her, both taunting and encouraging, as her mind ran over all the responses she'd rehearsed. None of them seemed adequate.

"I'm here because of Easton." It was the truth stripped of every excuse. She was here to atone for her debt to the family she'd wronged.

Pain lanced through the aging woman's gaze, twisting her fine-boned features with lines. Raw fury followed. "Do you want something from us, Ms. Maddox?" Condescension infused her drawling alto.

Not what you're thinking, that's for sure. I'm no gold-digger. "Yes. Very much. I want a job at Genesis." She could never restore Easton to his family, but she would offer herself in his place. She would spend the rest of her career serving their company in whatever capacity they would permit. It was the penance she'd chosen for herself.

The muscles around Waverly's mouth tightened a few degrees more. "Why not return to DRAW Corporation? To your own family?"

She refused to drop the elder woman's gaze as she absorbed each question, knowing they were shot like bullets to shatter her resolve, to remind her how unwelcome her presence was. She'd expected no other reception from the Calcagni dynasty; some would even argue she deserved this woman's scorn. However, she'd never been easily intimidated, a trait that was at times a strength and other times a curse. "With all due respect, Mrs. Calcagni, this *is* my family now."

Waverly's lips parted as if she would protest. Something akin to fear joined the choleric emotions churning across her countenance. She clamped her lips together, while her chest rose and fell several times. "You may take a seat now." She waved a heavily be-ringed hand to indicate the lounge area to her right. Lips pursed the skin around her mouth into papery creases, as she punched a few buttons on the call panel. "Ms. Maddox has arrived." Her frigid tone transformed each word into ice picks.

Jacey expelled the two painful clumps of air her lungs had been holding prisoner in a silent, drawn-out whoosh as she eased past the reception booth. She'd survived the first round of interrogations, a small triumph that yielded her no satisfaction. She knew the worst was yet to come. Waverly Calcagni was no more than a guard dog; Luca Calcagni was the one they sent into the boxing ring to finish off their opponents.

Luca apparently saw fit to allow her to marinate in her uneasiness past their appointment time. Not a surprise. He had the upper hand today and would do everything in his power to squash her with it. A full hour cranked away on the complicated maze of copper gears and chains on the wall. There was nothing ordinary about the interior of Genesis & Sons. Even their clocks were remarkable feats of architecture.

"Ms. Maddox? Mr. Calcagni is ready to see you."

She had to remind herself to breathe as she stood. At first she could see nothing but Luca's tall silhouette in the shadowed archway leading to the inner sanctum of Genesis & Sons. Then he took a step forward into a beam of sunlight and beckoned her to follow him. She stopped breathing again but somehow forced her feet to move in his direction.

He was everything she remembered and more from their few brief encounters. Much more. Up close, he seemed taller, broader, infinitely more intimidating, and so wickedly gorgeous it made her dizzy. That her parents had labeled him and his brothers as forbidden fruit made them all the more appealing to her during her teen years. It took her fascinated brain less than five seconds to recognize Luca had lost none of his allure.

The blue-black sheen of his hair, clipped short on the sides and longer on top, lent a deceptive innocence that didn't fool her one bit. Nor did the errant lock slipping to his forehead on one side. The expensive weave of his suit and complex twists of his tie far better illustrated his famed unpredictable temperament. His movements were controlled but fluid, bringing to her mind the restless prowl of a panther as she followed him down the hall and into an elevator. It shimmered with mirrored glass and recessed mahogany panels.

They rode in tense silence to the top floor.

Arrogance rolled off him from his crisply pressed white shirt, to his winking diamond and white gold cuff links, down to his designer leather shoes. In some ways, his arrogance was understandable. He guided the helm of one of the world's most profitable companies, after all. And his eyes! They were as beautiful and dangerous as the rest of him. Tawny with flecks of gold, they regarded her with open contempt as he ushered her from the elevator.

They entered a room surrounded by glass. One wall of windows overlooked the gulf waters. The other three framed varying angles of the Anchorage skyline. Gone was the old-world elegance of the first floor. This room was all Luca. A statement of power in chrome and glass. Sheer contemporary minimalism with no frills.

"Have a seat." It was an order, not an offer. A call to battle.

It was a battle she planned to win. She didn't want to consider the alternative — slinking back to her humble apartment in defeat.

He flicked one darkly tanned hand at the pair of Chinese Chippendale chairs resting before his expansive chrome desk. The chairs were stained black like the heart of their owner. No cushions.

They were not designed for comfort, only as a place to park guests whom the CEO did not intend to linger.

She planned to change his mind on that subject before her allotted hour was up. "Thank you." Without hesitation, she took the chair on the right, making no pretense of being in the driver's seat. This was his domain. Given the chance, she planned to mold herself into the indispensable right hand to whoever in the firm he was willing to assign her. On paper, she might not look like she had much to offer, but there was a whole pack of demons driving her. An asset he wouldn't hesitate to exploit once he recognized their unique value. Or so she hoped.

To her surprise, he didn't seat himself behind his executive throne. Instead, he positioned himself between her and his desk, hiking one hip on the edge and folding his arms. It was a deliberate invasion of her personal space with all six feet two of his darkly arresting half-Hispanic features and commanding presence.

Most women would have swooned.

Jacey wasn't most women. She refused to give him the satisfaction of either fidgeting or being the first to break the silence. Silence was a powerful weapon, something she'd learned at the knees of her parents. Prepared to use whatever it took to get what she'd come for, she allowed it to stretch well past the point of politeness.

Luca finally unfolded his arms and reached for the file sitting on the edge of his desk. "I read your application and resume. It didn't take long."

According to her mental tally, the first point belonged to her. She nodded to acknowledge his insult and await the next.

He dangled her file above the trash canister beside his desk and released it. It dropped and settled with a papery flutter.

"I fail to see how singing in nightclubs the past five years qualifies you for any position at Genesis & Sons."

The attack was so predictable she wanted to smile, but didn't dare. Too much was at stake. She'd made the mistake of taunting him with a smile once before. Nine years earlier. Hopefully, he'd long forgotten the ill-advised lark.

Or not. His golden gaze fixed itself with such intensity on her mouth that her insides quaked with uneasiness. Nine years later, he'd become harder and exponentially more ruthless. She'd be wise to remember it.

"Singing is one of art's most beautiful forms," she countered softly. "According to recent studies, scientists believe it releases endorphins and oxytocin while reducing cortisol." *There.* He wasn't the only one who'd been raised in a tank swimming with intellectual minds.

The tightening of his jaw was the only indication

her answer had caught him by surprise. Luca was a man of facts and numbers. Her answer couldn't have possibly displeased him, yet his upper lip curled. "If you came to sing for me, Ms. Maddox, I'm all ears."

The smile burgeoning inside her mouth vanished. Every note of music in her had died with her husband. That part of her life was over. "We both know I did not submit my employment application in the hopes of landing a singing audition." She started to rise, a calculated risk. "If you don't have any interest in conducting the interview you agreed to, I'll just excuse my—"

"Have a seat, Ms. Maddox." Her veiled suggestion of his inability to keep his word clearly stung.

She sat.

"Remind me what other qualifications you disclosed on your application. There were so few, they seem to have slipped my mind."

Nothing slipped his mind. She would bet all the money she no longer possessed on it. "A little forgetfulness is understandable, Mr. Calcagni. You're a very busy man."

Her dig hit home. This time the clench of his jaw was more perceptible.

Now that she had his full attention, she plunged on. "My strengths are in behind-the-scenes marketing as well as personal presentations. As you are well aware, I cut my teeth on DRAW Corporation's drafting tables. I'm proficient in an exhaustive list of software programs and a whiz at compiling slides, notes, memes, video clips, animated graphics, and most types of printed materials. My family just this morning offered to return me to my former position in marketing."

"Why would they do that?"

"They hoped to crown me Vice President of Communications in the next year or two. I believe their exact words were *it's my rightful place.*" As much as she tried to mask it, a hint of derision crept in her voice. There were plenty of employees on her family's staff who were far more qualified and deserving of the promotion.

His lynx eyes narrowed to slits. "You speak in the past tense, Ms. Maddox. After recalling what a flight risk you are, I presume your family withdrew their offer?"

It was a slap at her elopement with his brother. She'd figured he'd work his way around to it, eventually. "No." She deliberately bit her lower lip, testing him with another ploy that rarely failed in her dealings with men. "I turned them down."

His gaze locked on her mouth once more. Male interest flashed across his face and was gone. "Why?"

He was primed for the kill. She spread her hands and went for the money shot. "To throw myself at your complete mercy, Mr. Calcagni." The beauty of it was that the trembling in her voice wasn't faked; the request she was about to make was utterly genuine. "As your sister by marriage, I am not here to debate my qualifications or lack of them. I am begging you to give me a job. I need the income. I need to be busy. I'll take whatever position you are willing to offer so long as it allows me to come to work in this particular building." She whipped her face aside, no longer able to meet his gaze. "Here," she reiterated fiercely. "Where *he* doesn't feel as far away as he does outside these walls."

Because of the number of moments it took to compose herself, she missed his initial reaction to her words. When she tipped her face up to his once more, his expression was unreadable.

"Assuming everything you say is true, Ms. Maddox, and you're not simply up to another one of your games..." He paused, his tone indicating he thought she was guilty of the latter. "We do not currently have any job openings."

"That's not what your publicist claims, and it's certainly not what you have posted on your website." She dug through her memory to resurrect a segment of the Genesis creed. "Where innovation and vision collide. Where the world's most introspective minds are ever welcome—"

"Believe me, Ms. Maddox, I am familiar with our corporate creed. There is no need to repeat it. Especially since I have already made my decision concerning your employment."

Fear sliced through her. They were only five

minutes into her interview, and he was shutting her down. "Mr. Calcagni, I—"

He stopped her with an upraised hand. "You may start your two-week trial in the morning. Eight o'clock sharp."

He was actually offering her a job? Or, in this case, a ticket to the next round? According to her inner points tally, she hadn't yet accumulated enough to win. It didn't feel like a victory, either. She had either failed to read some of his cues, or he was better at hiding them than anyone else she'd ever encountered. She no longer had any idea where they stood with each other in their banter of words, who was winning and who was losing. It made her insides weaken to the consistency of jelly.

"Since we have no vacancies in the vice presidency category," he infused an ocean-sized dose of sarcasm into his words, "you'll be serving as my personal assistant. Like every other position on our payroll, it amounts to long hours, hard work, and no coddling. You're under no obligation to accept my offer, of course."

"I accept." She couldn't contain her smile this time. She didn't understand his game, but she'd achieved what she'd come for. Employment. No matter how humble the position. Sometimes it was best not to overthink things. "Thank you, Mr. Calcagni."

There was no answering warmth in him. "You won't be thanking me tomorrow."

"A risk I will gladly take." She rose to seal her commitment with a handshake and immediately realized her mistake.

Standing brought her nearly flush with her new boss. Close enough to catch a whiff of his aftershave — a woodsy musk with a hint of cobra slithering her way. Every organ in her body suffered a tremor beneath the full blast of his scrutiny.

When his long fingers closed over hers, her insides radiated with the same intrinsic awareness of him she'd experienced nine years ago — the day they first met.

It was a complication she hadn't counted on.

<<< *To be continued...* >>>

I hope you enjoyed this excerpt from
Her Billionaire Boss
*Available in eBook and paperback on Amazon +
FREE in Kindle Unlimited!*

Much love,
Jo

ABOUT JO

Jo is an Amazon bestselling author of sweet and inspirational romance stories about faith, hope, love and family drama with a few Texas-sized detours into comedy. She also writes sweet and inspirational historical romance as Jovie Grace.

1.) Follow on Amazon!
amazon.com/author/jografford

2.) Join Cuppa Jo Readers!
https://www.facebook.com/groups/
CuppaJoReaders

3.) Follow on Bookbub!

https://www.bookbub.com/authors/jo-grafford

4.) Follow on Instagram!
https://www.instagram.com/jografford/

5.) Follow on YouTube
https://www.youtube.com/channel/
UC3R1at97Qso6BXiBIxCjQ5w

amazon.com/authors/jo-grafford

bookbub.com/authors/jo-grafford

facebook.com/jografford

instagram.com/jografford

pinterest.com/jografford

Made in the USA
Middletown, DE
28 December 2022

20589901R00106